The Director's Cut

A Patricia Fisher Mystery

Book 3

Steve Higgs

Dedication

To Joanne Clover for suggesting the rather excellent name Jeremiah
Anthony Bumblethorpe

Table of Contents:

Battle on Board

The whoosh of flame leaping into the air made me jump just as the thump of the explosion that caused it reached my ears. It was so close I could feel the change of air pressure in my lungs. Across the deck, I watched as Barbie, dressed in a short, figure-hugging red cocktail dress and heels, cowered behind the bar of the upper deck sun terrace. Two bullets gouged holes in the bar next to her head, splinters flying off dangerously as she ducked back again. Her eyes showed the panic she felt.

'Stay there! I'm coming to you,' yelled a man's voice. My eyes swung to see where the voice had come from. Doug Douglas looked handsome in his black dinner suit, but the jacket and trousers had seen better days, ripped as they were on both knees and the sleeve of the jacket hanging open on his right shoulder. There was blood coming from a cut on his left cheek, but he looked more angry than scared.

He was crouching in a doorway that led back into the upper deck accommodation where I knew his suite was located. As he stood up to start across the deck, another explosion threw him across the deck and set fire to his jacket.

Barbie screamed, but stayed where she was, terrified that any movement might expose her to the shooter.

Doug Douglas rolled across the deck, flipped himself upright and with gritted teeth, he ripped the burning jacket from his body and cast it aside. Doing so revealed the twin holsters hung under his arms and as I stared in rapt fascination, he whipped them both out and began sprinting across the deck, guns raised in front of him as he fired shot after shot at a target I couldn't see.

A man dressed all in black and wearing a balaclava to hide his face, leapt down to the deck from a platform above the terrace. He landed neatly on both feet and was already shooting at Doug before he was fully standing again. The weapon in his hands was some kind of assault rifle - big and black and lethal looking.

Doug lined up his pair of pistols and shot him, the bullets both hitting the man in the chest to bowl him over backward. As the man went down, Doug Douglas leapt over his body and fired again as two more men dressed in black emerged from a doorway to his left.

Yet another explosion rocked the ship, knocking Doug off balance and he fell painfully to the deck as Barbie screamed yet again. He scrambled to put himself against a low wall filled with plants, part of the decoration on the sun terrace. Using the few seconds respite his cover gave, he ejected his empty magazines and reloaded ready for the next round.

I saw him check around, scanning everywhere for danger, then bounce to his feet and instantly start shooting again as five more targets appeared to his front. Bullets hit the deck all around him as he darted forward; it seemed impossible that he could avoid them all but just as I thought that, a puff of red exploded from his right shoulder and he faltered, throwing away his empty guns as he stumbled onward.

'I'm coming, baby!' he shouted above the deafening noise of the burning ship.

The black clad men were still coming though. One emerged from a doorway as Doug passed it. Too close for a gun, even if he had one, Doug grabbed the man's assault rifle, ripping it upward to strike him under the chin, then yanked it downward so the strap around his body pulled him off balance. There was a sickening crunch as he followed him down with an elbow to the back of his head, but Doug got no time to rest - another terrorist was coming!

This one had a knife which he thrust toward the hero, only to find Doug was no longer where he had been. Doug whipped a long leg around in an arc to kick the man in his ear. Holding his pose and balancing on one leg, he then kicked him in the jaw as his head rebounded, followed the kick through, and spun around into a crouch as he scanned for any further danger.

Satisfied that he was safe, for now at least, Doug Douglas stood up, walked across the ruined terrace, and offered Barbie his hand to get up.

Nervously smiling, she took it and he pulled her into an embrace.

'Doug, you're hurt,' she cried, terror making her voice wobble.

'They're just scratches, babe. Nothing compared with the pain I would feel if I lost you.'

'Oh, Doug,' she swooned.

He kissed her then, amidst the madness and destruction, he folded her back as he leaned into her, and stole her breath with his manliness.

As he broke the kiss and brought her back to her feet, a voice rang out from behind him.

'Mr Douglas, did you really think it would be that easy?'

Doug spun around to face his enemy.

'Doctor Enviro, why don't you stop this madness? Or do I have to stop you?' he narrowed his eyes, squinting at an arch-rival who simply refused to die.

Doctor Enviro walked into view. Armed with a powerful looking rifle and wary enough to keep his distance from Doug Douglas, he nevertheless had the upperhand.

Doug wasn't armed and once again Barbie looked utterly terrified.

Doctor Enviro laughed. It sounded evil and false, but as its mirth ended, he said, 'I think it is time I taught you a lesson for interfering in my affairs.' Then he pulled the trigger on his giant gun, startling Doug as he moved to protect Barbie. He was too late though. The shot had hit her just below her perfect left breast.

She had time to utter a single word, 'Doug,' as she fell, the handsome hero catching her before she hit the deck. She looked into his eyes for a moment then, as my heart stopped from the spectacle I was witnessing, her head lolled back.

Behind him, Doctor Enviro cackled.

'Cut!'

A spontaneous round of applause accompanied by whoops and whistles burst from the crowd of onlookers jammed in behind the barriers as I wiped a tear from my eye. Doug Douglas adjusted his stance then lifted Barbie back on to her feet, stealing a quick peck on her cheek as he did. He was saying something to her, her hands in his as he held her gaze. It looked like he was being complimentary about her acting which was the right thing to do - she was amazing.

Then he dropped one of her hands and turned to the still applauding crowd and took a deep bow, pulling Barbie with him as if they were both on stage in a West End theatre.

They were still bowing as members of the special effects coordination team rushed the set with fire extinguishers. They made the set safe and checked all the pyrotechnics had gone off correctly. As they busied themselves, Doug escorted Barbie toward the director.

The Aurelia, the world's largest and finest cruise ship, had set sail from Los Angeles, California five days ago. The three-day, two-night stay in California had been eventful but not in a good way. Unless you like being involved in murder mysteries and having people point guns at you. If you like that sort of thing, it would have been fun. Before we arrived in LA, I had heard a vague rumour about a film crew coming aboard but hadn't paid any attention to what people were saying. When we came back on board though, the upper deck of the ship was being transformed into a film set and there was a distinct buzz going around the crew and the passengers. Hollywood A-Listers Tarquin Trebeck and Bhavana Navuluri were coming on board to film sequences from their new film, the as yet unnamed follow up to their blockbuster hit *Game of Fools*. Tarquin would play tough guy Doug Douglas, a role he seemed suited to with his broad shoulders and square jaw.

I hadn't paid much attention to the actors, the stars or the unknown supporting cast but my butler had been getting very excited about it all, talking about what they were doing and who he had seen, and I indulged his chatter quite happily because he was rarely this animated. However, on the second day at sea, the young woman they had on board to play Doug Douglas's ill-fated girlfriend, had one champagne too many, slipped by the pool and broke her ankle. She never made it in front of the camera, but before the shoot ground to a halt, Tarquin Trebeck pulled Barbie from the crowd and asked if she could have a go at acting.

I certainly wasn't surprised by his choice; Barbie is the kind of girl you see on the cover of Sports Illustrated's swim wear edition. She was simply stunning, with a perfect smile, high cheek bones and flowing natural blonde hair. They did a few screen tests and I watched as the makeup boy moved in to adjust her face, pursed his lips a few times and declared her ready without so much as taking out a brush.

That was two days ago, and she had filmed several scenes since. They said they might need to go back and refilm a scene later but otherwise her character was now dead, and her death was to act as the catalyst for Doug Douglas's rage to follow.

Just across from me, the director called a wrap for the day and hopped out of his folding chair to shake Tarquin's hand. Barbie spotted me and bounded across to wrap me up in a hug. 'Oh, my goodness, Patty, this has been so exciting. I can't believe the captain let me do it.' She was gushing with excitement but let me go to grab my staid butler and give him the same treatment.

I knew Jermaine was doing his very best to keep a lid on his own excitement, but it bubbled over now. 'Barbie, you were amazing!'

'You really were,' I agreed.

Barbie's overstimulated brain was bouncing from one thought to the next. 'I can't wait to watch the dailies later. I wonder if they will need me to refilm any scenes?'

Jermaine nudged her hip. 'Do you mean you hope they refilm the scene where you have to make out with Tarquin?' he teased.

Barbie's cheeks blushed bright red. 'Maybe,' she giggled. 'He is awfully handsome. And he's single and he is ever such a gentleman.'

Jermaine made his eyes bug out at her in fake surprise. 'You mean he hasn't tried to...'

'Certainly not,' she cut him off before he could complete his sentence. 'He has asked if I am joining the rest of the film crew for dinner tonight though.'

'I thought you were invited anyway, because you are part of the film crew?' I asked.

'Well, yes,' replied Barbie. 'But it was nice of him to make sure I was coming. I think he wants me to sit with him.'

'Madam, it sounds like there is a romance blooming, wouldn't you say?' Jermaine's comment made her face blush again.

But she grinned and said, 'I need to get this dress off, the blood bag has made me all sticky. I'll come by your room later, if that's okay? We can go to dinner together.'

It sounded good to me. 'Yes, I suppose this is your first time having dinner as a guest at one of the captain's table events.'

Barbie nodded her head vigorously. 'I never expected to eat in the upper deck restaurant at all. So few staff ever do unless they rise to very senior positions. It's not the venue I'm excited about though...'

'It's the company,' Jermaine finished with another grin.

Barbie stuck her tongue out at him, the two friends ribbing each other just for fun. I was glad to share in her good fortune and hoped it might continue. She had to go though; I had no doubt the burst blood bag was unpleasant, so I congratulated her again and watched as she headed back to chat with some of the film crew and get the pyrotechnic patch thing under her dress removed. She was giddy with happiness, and I couldn't blame her.

'It is almost four o'clock, madam, would you care for some tea?' asked Jermaine, his reserved butler's tone firmly back in place.

I smiled as I said, 'Yes, Jermaine, tea would be suitable.'

'Very good, madam. I will prepare for your return.' He started walking away, but as I turned to follow him, seeing nothing to keep me here any longer and keen to return to the mystery novel I had been reading, I bumped into a short, rather sweaty, little man with a bushy beard.

'Gosh,' he said as he bounced off me and fell to the deck. He rolled over and bounced back onto his feet as if he were made of rubber. 'Terribly sorry,' he said as he straightened his glasses. 'I really ought to look where I am going.'

'That's perfectly alright,' I assured him. Jermaine heard the commotion the man made and returned to check whether his assistance was required.

The man was distracted by his left hand though. He had cut it on something when he fell over. 'Oh, God. I think I'm going to be sick,' he said and then keeled over right in front of me.

'Did he just faint?' asked Jermaine as he came to stand next to me. We both looked down but he was coming around again before we could react.

'Goodness. Sorry about that. Might one of you have a tissue?' he asked, sitting up now but still on the deck. 'I really cannot stand the sight of blood.'

Ever resourceful, Jermaine pulled a pack of tissues from one of his many pockets, handed them over and then gave the man a hand to pull him upright once more. The short man looked at me and then at Jermaine and then back at me and then his jaw dropped. 'Wait a second,' he started, 'I know you. You're the lady that solved the Kristina Khymera murder case. I saw you on TV.' Then he looked at Jermaine. 'And you're her butler. Oh, my goodness, you're Melissa Fleischer!'

'Patricia Fisher,' I corrected him.

'Yeah, that's what I meant,' he said. 'Wow. Everywhere I turn, there are famous people.'

The man was just staring at us, open mouthed and a little like a lost dog. To move things along politely, I asked, 'Are you part of the film crew?'

'Me? Yeah. I'm with the special effects firm,' he boasted proudly. 'I had probably better go actually, lots to do and all.' He grinned, shrugged and hurried away.

'Famous,' I echoed to myself as I started walking back to my suite. Now that was a strange concept. I hadn't realised we had been on TV. Sure, there had been cameras when we left Kristina's property, and I answered a few questions. It hadn't occurred to me that it would be broadcast or that someone would identify me though.

Since I came on board the Aurelia twenty-three days ago, my life had become a whirlwind of exotic destinations, life changing experiences and all too frequent adrenalin fuelled chases. My name is Patricia Fisher, and I am still trying to wrap my head around the shift from the person I was the day I caught my husband cheating on me with my best friend, to the person I am today. Something shifted internally during my first few days on board, when, accused of murder and embroiled in a decades old priceless jewel theft, I somehow rediscovered myself hidden beneath the shabby frame of Charlie Fisher's wife.

Serendipity, fate, luck, call it what you wish, I had gone from being a woman whose best days had passed her by and who cleaned houses to earn money she didn't need, to being the lady staying in the royal suite on board the world's finest luxury cruise ship. I knew the captain by name, I had my own butler and somewhere along the line, I had tripped over the truth about the stolen jewel and ended up with a fat reward. I made friends along the way, but the transient nature of passengers on board the ship meant that they never stayed for long.

Back in my suite, Jermaine served tea with finger-size cucumber, smoked salmon and cream cheese sandwiches while I quietly read to pass some time. In a few hours, I would attend a gala dinner and sit at the captain's table. The dinners were a weekly event, but this one had been thrown in as an extra in deference to the big-name Hollywood actors. Barbie was coming for the first time, but the captain's table was a regular haunt for me. So regular, in fact, that I needed to ask someone about it. Most guests would receive an invitation to the captain's table dinner but very few actually got to sit at his table. Rather, they got to be in the room and enjoy the ambiance. Seats at his table were a rare commodity reserved for visiting royalty, famous people and those staying in the most expensive suites. I qualified due to the last factor, but even so, I should expect one invite per month at best. Instead, I was there every time an event was held, and someone had to be orchestrating that.

I was interested to learn who it was.

Tarquin had indeed wanted Barbie to sit with him, or someone had arranged it so that would happen. Barbie hadn't known, of course, but she was met at the door of the upper deck exclusive restaurant when we arrived and escorted to her seat so that she knew where it was. There were labels on the chairs; the one next to hers was Tarquin's.

It was normal practice for the captain to host dinner on a Saturday night and that was the case this time but the buzz in the room was all about the film stars and the famous director on board. Crew were circulating with glasses of champagne, though Barbie stuck with water as was her normal habit; her life as a gym instructor dictated that she followed a very clean and healthy lifestyle. I indulged though as we chatted about whether she might want to pursue a career in acting now that she would be seen by millions on screen for the first time.

'I don't know, Patty,' she replied. 'It's a really big decision. It all looks so glamorous, but I think the people that achieve that lifestyle sacrifice their privacy and so many of them have a string of failed relationships behind them that I would be terrified it might happen to me too.'

It was a valid point. I presented a counter argument though. 'Not all of them do. I bet we can come up with plenty of examples of famous couples that have stayed together for life if we try. I suspect it pays rather well too.'

She inclined her head in agreement. 'That it does. Do you know what Tarquin is being paid for this film?' When I shook my head, she leaned in to whisper a number in my ear. 'Isn't that obscene?' she added afterward when she saw my eyes widen.

'It certainly is a lot more than I expected,' I agreed.

'Ooh, here they come.' Barbie was straining her neck to see over and around the press of people in front of us as the captain entered the room with an entourage of senior officers and all the invited members of film crew. I noted that it wasn't every member of the film crew joining us; just by numbers I could tell there were lots missing. Not that I knew how many film crew were on board but it had to be close to one hundred and less than fifty came into the room. They were being led by Tarquin, but beside him was the leading lady of the film, Bhavana Navuluri, a stunningly beautiful Indian woman with jet black hair and a figure to rival any supermodel on the planet. I hadn't seen the first film and hadn't yet seen her act in this one, but I was given to believe that she wasn't nearly as talented as she was attractive. In fact, what I heard was derogatory comments and questions regarding how she managed to land the roles she got.

Behind them, and chatting with the film's director, Paul Deacon, was a small man I hadn't seen before. He wore a turtleneck sweater beneath a tweed jacket, had a receding widow's peak and round wire-rimmed glasses. He looked more like an accountant than a film star. 'Who's the man next to the director?' I asked Barbie.

Barbie said, 'Oh, that's Ian Kenyon, he's the producer. He's um, he's not very nice.'

'Really? In what way?'

Barbie pursed her lips as she thought about her response. 'He's very gruff. I think he is just unpleasant to everyone, but he is always grumbling about money and that the film is going to go way over budget. He was complaining about Tarquin's fee yesterday. I overheard him say it would be more profitable to have him killed and get the insurance payout.' She laughed as she said it, a sort of nervous noise that betrayed how she felt about the handsome film star now approaching.

12

Tarquin Trebeck spotted Barbie, and his smile, which seemed always to be in place unless he was acting, broadened as he made a beeline for her. I had to admit; he was a good-looking man. A couple of inches over six feet tall, with a chiselled jaw and a mop of dark brown hair that complimented his twinkling blue eyes, he was the complete package. It also didn't hurt that he clearly spent a good few hours in the gym each week.

He all but jogged the last few meters to my friend, but where I, and I think Barbie also, expected him to take her hand and maybe peck her on the cheek, he pulled her into a very public embrace and kissed her full on the lips.

I saw Barbie's surprise, but she offered no resistance and I remembered that they had already kissed several times for the camera. This time though, in this setting, it was like a public declaration. The room had fallen silent for a second though the background hum of conversation started again once he broke the kiss and took her hand instead.

Looking into her eyes, Tarquin said, 'You look radiant, Barbie. Simply stunning. The camera deserves you.' She blushed deeply and looked at the floor. 'I'm sorry, it wasn't my intention to embarrass you,' he said, an apologetic grin teasing the corners of his mouth.

The accountant looking man, Ian Kenyon, passed behind him on his way to find his seat, but as he got close enough, he commented loud enough for anyone within a few metres to hear, 'Just bed her and move on will you, Tarquin? There's no need for all the effort; you can see she can't wait to get her panties off.'

Barbie's jaw dropped at the open insult, but she didn't have to respond, Tarquin released her hand and spun around to grab the man by his throat. Instantly, Ian Kenyon found he was balancing on his toes as the much larger, far stronger man lifted him off the floor by one hand. 'Apologise to the lady,' he demanded though clenched teeth, the words coming out as a threat.

'Not a chance, pretty boy,' the producer hissed back. 'Let go of me right now. You're not so famous you can't be sacked. Try working again once I get through telling the industry how impossible you are to work with.' While he delivered his threats, Ian was scrambling for purchase on Tarquin's hand, trying fruitlessly to prise his fingers off.

'Let him go, Tarquin.' The new voice was that of the director, Paul Deacon. His instruction was spoken softly but was no less insistent for it. Tarquin glared at him for a second, then slowly let the smaller man go.

The tension in the room was palpable; hundreds of faces were looking at Tarquin, Paul, Ian, and Barbie, but only Barbie seemed to notice. Perhaps the others were just used to continuous scrutiny.

Sensing her discomfort, Tarquin turned to her and offered his arm. He was going to walk away and be done with it, but Ian wasn't willing to let it go yet. 'That's right, pretty boy, walk away. Wouldn't want to get that perfect face bruised.'

Tarquin froze and I saw his lips moving as he wrestled with his decision. Reaching one, he turned to Barbie, said, 'Won't be a moment, dear,' and exploded into action. He reversed his direction, shooting back toward Ian Kenyon, who had dismissed the actor and started walking away himself. I thought Tarquin was going to punch him or kick him from behind, but instead he grabbed him around the waist, upended the smaller man, and ripped off his trousers!

As Tarquin stood up triumphantly waving Ian's trousers above his head and laughing, there was a pregnant pause, but then a woman laughed and pointed, and it started a ripple as more and more people began to laugh.

It became uncontrollable; so much so that I had to work hard to suppress my own mirth.

Ian Kenyon wasn't wearing any underwear and his tiny todger was on display for all to see. The poor man went bright red as he tried to cover himself. A nearby crewman in white livery handed him his hat for modesty, but it was way too late for that. Ian scrambled to his feet and pushed through the crowd, desperate to get away from everyone and the laughter they couldn't control.

As he ran, he shouted, 'This isn't over, Trebeck! You mark my words; I'm going to make you pay!'

Paul the director tapped Tarquin on his shoulder. 'That was not cool, Tarquin. Ian is going to hold a grudge forever. You have made shooting the rest of this film harder for everyone.'

'Just get a new producer, Paul,' Tarquin shot back. He wasn't feeling sorry about his actions and wasn't about to apologise for them. If anything, he looked to be having a great evening now. But when he turned to Barbie, he said, 'I'm terribly sorry about that, dear lady. I'm sure it would have been more mature of me to ignore him, but I cannot abide men insulting ladies. His words were unjustified.' He reached out to offer his arm to her once more. 'Now that he has gone, we should be in for a good time. Let's eat.'

Barbie looked relieved that the moment was done, but also embarrassed by all the negative attention Tarquin had drawn. She smiled a little nervously, then took Tarquin's arm and went with him to their table. I was sitting on a different table tonight though I probably could have used my status as the resident of the Windsor Suite to get a place on the captain's table had I wanted to. I had been a guest at the big table plenty of times already, and there were so many new people on board to meet, so I was happily taking a chair at a table just behind them as I watched Tarquin, ever the gentleman, pull out Barbie's chair for her.

Thankfully, the next hour passed without incident as the wait staff delivered course after course of sumptuous food from around the world. Guiltily, I stole a few glances in Barbie's direction. I was curious about what was going to happen between her and Tarquin. Not that I wanted details, of course. I had come to view her more as a daughter over the last month. I was certainly old enough to be her mother and she had a well-hidden fragile side that suggested she had been burned badly by relationships in the past. If she and Tarquin hit it off, what would happen when we arrived in Hawaii and he left the ship? My concern was that he would just move on but pretend that his intention was to do otherwise so that Barbie would be more inclined to give herself to his advances.

She wasn't a child though, and she certainly wasn't my child, so if I thought that was the way it was going, I wouldn't intervene. At least that was what I was telling myself. They were being relatively tactile with each other; holding hands beneath the table and sitting with his arm around her shoulders. He was handsome enough that he could have his pick of women and when you combined his looks with the fame and money, well... he was a catch if you could indeed catch him.

When five courses had been served and all the plates cleared to leave us with nothing but drinks at our tables, the lights in the great restaurant were dimmed and the entertainment began. A string quartet had been playing throughout dinner, their wonderful, sensual overtures the perfect accompaniment to polite dinner table conversation, but as a much louder band started playing covers of recent hits on the stage at the far end of the room, I felt a gentle tap on my shoulder.

I turned, expecting to find the gentlemen sitting next to me in want of something. His name was Micka and he was Swedish. His English was

16

pretty good, as I had discovered most Scandinavians to be, and he was taking a well-earned post retirement cruise with his wife of forty-two years. It wasn't Micka that had touched my bare shoulder though, it was the captain. Turning to look at Micka's face had simply put the captain's groin in my eyeline.

As I looked up, he sat down into the chair that Micka had vacated as his wife dragged him to the dancefloor. 'Good evening, Mrs Fisher,' the captain offered with a smile.

Now level with my face, it was easier to see his smile and return it as I said, 'Good evening, Captain.' We were of similar age, though he had worn better than I and did not look anywhere near his reported fifty-four years.

He dropped the smile to give me a serious expression. 'I just wanted to take a moment to apologise for not finding space for you at the head table this evening,' he said.

Surprised by his apology, I said, 'That's perfectly alright. I had no expectation that I would be on the head table.' Then, because his statement had made me curious, I said, 'I thought attendance at the captain's table was rotated evenly among as many passengers as possible.'

I had framed it as a question even though it wasn't. 'Well, yes,' the captain stuttered. Was he blushing? In the low lighting I couldn't tell for certain, but he was also acting as if embarrassed. It was completely out of character and I had to wonder what was happening. 'It is my prerogative to oversee the guest list and create the right balance of guests at my table. As the lady in the Windsor Suite you have certain additional rights...' he trailed off as if unsure how to end the sentence.

Sensing that he was floundering, I jumped in, touching his hand where it rested on the table when I said, 'It's really not a big deal, Alistair. I have eaten at your table plenty of times already, probably more than I was entitled to. It is very good of you to grant me special treatment because I am travelling alone, but there is really no need. And certainly no need to apologise when you cannot.'

In response, the handsome middle-aged man bowed his head in thought, then looked back up when he said, 'No one calls me Alistair.' Oh, God, I had stepped in some invisible etiquette landmine and insulted him when he was being ever so sweet. But as he saw my expression change to one of embarrassed horror, he quickly raised a hand to stop me speaking, 'No. I like it.' He reassured me with a lopsided grin. 'It's just… unexpected. You are unexpected, Mrs Fisher.' Before I could ask what that comment meant, he took my hand and kissed it gently, his trim whiskers tickling the skin as they passed. 'I'm afraid I must return to my table, Mrs Fisher. Perhaps we shall have a chance to speak again soon.' Then, with a curt nod, he was gone.

I was lost in thought for a moment, confused by the exchange, but when I allowed my eyes to focus across the table, I saw that several couples were staring at me. It looked like they were talking about me, speculating perhaps and one lady, who had to be in her late eighties at least, winked and gave me a knowing smile that made me wonder what everyone else thought they had just seen. They all clearly thought there was something going on between the captain and me, which there wasn't, but I wasn't going to waste my time explaining it to them.

Instead, I looked across to see what Barbie was up to but neither she nor Tarquin were in their seats. Guessing they were on the dancefloor, I looked for them there. Striking out, I looked around the room but the best-looking couple of the ship were nowhere to be seen. They had snuck out! Well, good for them: someone was getting lucky tonight.

I checked my watch and decided it was too early to return to my suite, so I left my seat and walked to the bar. There was waiter service at the table, but I had endured enough of being the only single person there. Everyone was too polite to ask me why I was travelling alone, which I was thankful for, but I was travelling alone and being around all those happy couples just hammered home how badly my own marriage had ended.

What I was currently lacking was a partner in crime. During my first month on board, I had made a couple of friends; women I could steal away from their husbands to visit the spa or have a womanly discussion about life over a cocktail. One such friend was Lady Mary Bostihill-Swank, a titled Lady from England who had left the ship with her famous author husband in LA. She and I had got into quite the scrape with some gangsters who boarded the ship in Miami. We met over dinner, the night she came aboard, finding mutual connections that made us firm friends very quickly. Now she was gone from the ship, leaving a hole that I needed to fill. We promised to stay in touch, and I swore I would look her up once I was back in England in late September.

At the bar, I ordered a stiff gin and tonic, raised a silent salute to Lady Mary and downed it in three swift hits. It still felt early to be leaving, but I was ready to go. Feeling a little melancholy from my loneliness, I tucked my clutch under my arm and left the restaurant: it was time for bed.

'Good morning, madam.' I was greeted by Jermaine as I came into the living area of my suite yawning as I went. He was attired in his black butler's uniform, pressed and starched and immaculate and he was arranging flowers to go into an ornate crystal vase when I joined him. His cabin was adjoined to mine through a door in the kitchen so that he was always at hand. There were push buttons in most rooms for the occupants to summon him, though I had never felt the need to use them after the very first time when curiosity demand I press one to see what happened.

The suite was vast and had more rooms than I could work out what to do with. My husband, whom I was recently separated from after I caught him in bed with my best friend, earned good money and had bought a nice house in the country. By comparison though, it was tiny next to the Windsor Suite. Jermaine kept it spotless for me, doing much of the tidying himself, though I knew he brought a cleaning crew in whenever I went out. He tried to ensure I was not inconvenienced by any of the mundane function in life, but I had walked in on them making my bed or vacuuming under my couches. It was testament to his efficiency that I had only ever seen them a few times in over three weeks on board.

'May I prepare something special for breakfast, madam?' he asked as he handed me a sports drink bottle filled with cool water.

Intrigued, I asked, 'What do you have in mind?'

He twitched his eyebrows twice to indicate that he was up to no good and leaned down so his head was closer to mine and could whisper. 'I secured a supply of Dungeness crab, madam. I can prepare crab eggs Benedict upon your return.'

I was about to go to the gym, my routine of getting some early morning exercise a habit that started when I first came aboard. At the time I had been berating myself for gaining unnecessary pounds but had soon realised that I was comfortable as I was. The exercise made me feel stronger though, more flexible and capable, so I was continuing with it and I had lost a few pounds along the way as a result. Crab eggs Benedict was on no one's diet list, but it sure sounded good and I was about to burn some calories. Jermaine waited patiently while I argued with myself, but in the end, taste won over waistline concerns and I gave him a nod while telling myself I would do an extra fifteen minutes on the stepper.

Yeah, that didn't happen. I could hear the sound of voices long before I turned into the passage that held the entrance door to the upper deck gym. The early morning nature of my workout dictated that very few other people were ever around. I liked not having to share equipment and space with others, and also that I didn't have to think too much about being the old, out of shape one in the gym. There was something going on this morning though; I could see people through the frosted glass of the door, more of them than I should expect to see this early, but as I pushed the door open, I saw that they were not there to use the gym.

A dozen faces turned to see who was coming in and a hand came up to halt my advance, the man nearest the door taking it upon himself to stop me. 'I'm afraid the gym is temporarily out of use,' he said. 'You can utilise the gym on the next deck down though.'

Further into the room, someone countermanded his instructions. 'That won't be necessary. Mrs Fisher, good morning,' I heard the familiar voice of Mr Ikari, the ship's deputy captain and head of security. He emerged from between two taller guards who had obscured him from my view, but it was the next voice that caught my attention.

'Patty?' Behind all the men in their white uniforms, Barbie was hidden somewhere. 'Patty, is that you?'

The guards parted so she could see me, revealing a tear-streaked face and a puffy red nose. Surprised and worried about what might have caused her to be upset, I rushed to her, wrapping her into a hug as she clung to me.

'What happened?' I asked, my voice a calm, soothing hush that she could relax into.

'Someone booby trapped my locker,' she blubbed, barely getting the words out between sobs.

Mr Ikari took over, 'Miss Berkeley had quite a scare this morning, Mrs Fisher. Someone broke into the gym, forced her locker open and fitted it with a blade on a spring hinge before closing it again.' He pointed across the room and I gasped as I saw a kitchen knife buried to its hilt in the wall opposite her locker. 'The blade was intended to do harm. Miss Berkeley was lucky that she was not standing in front of the locker when she opened it.'

'I could have been killed,' she wailed. 'Who would want to kill me, Patty?'

I had no answer, but Mr Ikari took my arm, urging me to follow him. Curious, I stood up again, letting Barbie go as one of the guards brought her a cup of tea. Mr Ikari inclined his head toward the door; he wanted to speak to me outside.

'There is something else I need to tell you,' he said as the gym door swung shut. Then he waited until he was sure he had my attention and said, 'This may come as a shock.'

That simple warning had my brain whirling. What on earth was he about to reveal? 'Spit it out please, Mr Ikari.'

He sighed, then took in a deep breath. 'At half past two this morning, a roving patrol from the ship's security discovered Mr Trebeck in the upper deck pool.'

'That doesn't sound too terrible,' I replied. Then wondered, 'Was he skinny dipping? Was he skinny dipping with Barbie?'

Mr Ikari looked confused by my questions, but said, 'Um, no, Mrs Fisher. His throat had been cut. He was floating.'

I gasped. 'Oh, my goodness! He was murdered?' As soon as the question left my lips, I realised how ridiculous it sounded. Of course, he had been murdered, he couldn't have cut his own throat. 'Does Barbie know?'

With his head bowed, Mr Ikari said, 'Not yet.'

'This is bad. This is really, really bad.' I was holding my face, too stunned at the news to know what to think. 'We have to tell her,' I concluded. 'It will be much worse if she finds out later.'

'I know,' replied Mr Ikari sadly. 'I was made aware of her... friendship with Mr Trebeck by one the crew this morning and was on my way to speak with her when I heard about the booby trap in her locker. It would seem that I have some detective work to perform.' Mr Ikari did not look excited by the task and there was no reason why he should. We were on board a luxury cruise liner; one might reasonably expect that the worst crime would be petty theft from one of the shops. Murder on board seemed surprisingly common though. He straightened himself as if preparing for the task, then asked, 'Would you like to stay with her, while I deliver the news?' It was clear by his tone that he thought it a good idea.

It was the sort of news one gave while the bereaved person's close female relatives were present. I would have to do.

I took the lead, going ahead of him to claim the seat next to Barbie. Taking her hand, I said, 'Mr Ikari has some news to share with you, Barbie. I'm afraid it might be difficult to listen to.'

Still reeling from the shock of the knife in her locker, Barbie's bewildered eyes turned up to look at the deputy captain. 'What is it?' she asked. I squeezed her hand as he delivered the shocking news of Tarquin Trebeck's death and waited for her to dissolve. No tears came though, she merely nodded and said, 'Was it an accident?'

'Um, no,' replied Mr Ikari who then went on to explain how the multimillion-dollar, Hollywood A-lister actor had been killed. When he finished, he asked, 'Can I have you escorted back to your cabin, Miss Berkeley?'

I shot him a look. 'I think perhaps my suite would be a better location. You can be with friends there; much better than being alone in your cabin.' Mr Ikari nodded his thanks. He hadn't considered what she might do once they had delivered her safely to her quarters.

Barbie had other ideas though. She let go of my hand and stood up, forcefully sniffing and wiping her eyes as she put on a smile that fooled no one. 'I have clients coming to the gym today. I have been away from my job for days due to filming but it's time to come back to reality. If you could have your men check there are no further deadly boobytraps fitted anywhere, Mr Ikari, I believe I would like to get on with my day.'

'Are you sure, Barbie?' I asked as I too stood up.

'Yes, Patty. I won't achieve anything by moping, whether that is done in my cabin or your suite. I think I will be best served by keeping busy. Don't you agree?' she asked.

I didn't agree, but I believed it would be best to let her come to terms with what had happened in her own way. I offered her a smile and patted her shoulder. She was already moving though, heading back behind the counter to start up the computer; going about her day as if nothing had happened.

Mr Ikari already had men checking over the gym equipment and the rest of the lockers when I arrived. He declared the gym to be all clear, but he hadn't finished with Barbie. As his men departed, he asked two of his lieutenants to wait by the door. 'Miss Berkeley, I'm afraid I have to ask you a few questions about the nature of your relationship with Mr Trebeck and your movements last night.'

She stopped moving and stared at him for a second. Then she nodded curtly. 'Of course, sir. You want to know if I was sleeping with him and if I killed him.'

He didn't smile at her directness, but he said, 'Indeed, Miss Berkeley. These are things that I need to know.'

Barbie folded her arms. It was a protective action I had seen her perform many times. She probably wasn't aware that she did it, but it told me that she was uncomfortable even though she was acting like the questions didn't bother her. 'I can report that I have not had sex with Tarquin Trebeck.' I can honestly say that her claim surprised me. 'I am quite certain it was his intention to bed me last night. His timing was off though, I have my period, so desire or otherwise on my part was not a factor. As for his murder; I left the party with him and he escorted me to the crew elevator where I kissed him goodnight. That was a shade after midnight, and I did not see him again.' She fell silent for a few seconds and looked at the countertop she was standing behind, then looked up again to say, 'And now I never will.'

Mr Ikari took his hat from beneath his left arm. 'Thank you, Miss Berkeley. If you think of anything else, please let me know.' He nodded a salute in my direction as he bid me a good day, then left the gym, his two lieutenants falling into place behind him.

'Shall we get started?' asked Barbie as she pushed her way into the gymnasium's cardio room.

I had one more go at talking her down off the emotional ledge, 'Are you sure you want to work today, Barbie? No one would think less of you if you took a few hours off.' I was genuinely worried about how little emotion she was displaying. Then I saw the crack in her armour as her bottom lip wobbled. Then her face folded completely, and we drew stares from the other people in the gym as she collapsed into me, sobs coming with ragged breaths. I let her get it all out, waving off one of the other instructors when he started towards us.

I could see that I wasn't going to get much done today, but it was more important to give my time to my friend. She needed me. So, it was to my great surprise when she let out a final shuddering gasp and prised herself away from me. Her face was a mess, but she was bringing herself under control again and had something to say, 'I want to find the man that did this.'

I opened my mouth to say something but couldn't work out what it was I wanted to say.

'The murderer, I mean. Not whoever put the knife in my locker. Unless it was the same person. Do you think it was the same person?' she was babbling now.

26

'Let's go to my suite,' I interrupted her, getting a word in quickly.

It stopped her mid-sentence. Then she snatched up my hand and dragged me to the door saying, 'Yes, that sounds sensible. Let's go.' I had just enough reaction time to snag my handbag as we went to the door.

It wasn't far to my suite though Barbie was silent on the way. I fished about in my handbag for the electronic keycard but as we turned the last corner, I saw that the door to my suite was open and there was a man standing outside of it.

As we drew closer, I heard what he was saying. 'It really is imperative that I speak with Mrs Fisher.' He was peering into the room beyond the door and darting his head about as if trying to catch a glimpse of what was inside.

No doubt Jermaine was blocking his path, but he was hidden from view inside the suite though we heard his voice when he answered, 'I have already advised you, sir; the lady of the house is not currently at home. You may return later at a more decent hour and I will, at that point, pass on your request to speak with her.' There was no emotion in his voice, just an immovable resistance.

'I know it's early, but this cannot wait.' replied the man outside my suite. 'I have to...'

'You have to what?' I asked, surprising the man and Jermaine both. Jermaine leaned forward to look outside, catching sight of me instantly and the man spun around toward the voice, a word he was about to say dying on his lips only to be replaced by another one as he recognised me.

I recognised him too. It was the short beardy man from the film set yesterday afternoon; the one that had known about Kristina's murder in Los Angeles. I held up my hand before he could say anything, speaking forcefully when I said, 'My friend needs some time without disturbance. Please call again later today.' Jermaine glanced at Barbie but did not ask what was wrong. Since she was too naturally attractive to bother with makeup, the only trace that she had been crying was a slight redness to her eyes and nostrils.

He returned his eyes to Jermaine who slowly folded his arms to make himself look a touch meaner and stared down at him with almost a foot of extra height. The man wasn't cowed though. He stamped his foot. 'No! That simply isn't good enough. A man has been murdered and I know who did it and someone is going to listen to me.' He was all but shouting and beginning to get emotional in his frustration.

I nodded at Jermaine. 'I think we had better take this inside. Perhaps some tea is in order.'

'I have breakfast prepared, madam,' Jermaine pointed out. He was so proud of what he did, and I was ruining it again.

Apologetically, I asked, 'Can you stretch it to feed everyone?'

The slightest flicker of annoyance played across his face before he recovered. 'Of course, madam. Shall I set a table on the terrace?'

We were inside the suite now, the door closing behind me as I followed Barbie inside. The short beardy man had gone through the lobby to find himself in the suite's main living area where he had come to a stop and was now looking around in startled bewilderment. 'The terrace would be lovely, thank you, Jermaine,' I replied as I too went through to the living room.

'My goodness,' breathed the man. 'How rich are you?'

'That is an impertinent question,' chided Jermaine, once again positioning himself in front of the man. 'Please state your name so I may announce you and mind your manners, please.'

'Announce me...' the man repeated what Jermaine had said but he was struggling to work out what it meant. 'Oh, you mean; what is my name? I'm Shane Sussmann. Don't you remember? We met yesterday.'

'You spoke to us yesterday but did not give your name despite knowing mine and that of Mrs Fisher.' Jermaine was telling the man off for his poor manners, but the message was too subtle for the man to understand.

Growing impatient to hear what he knew, I interrupted. 'Shane, please sit with me and tell me all about what you believe you know.' I crossed the room to a pair of couches that were arranged either side of a coffee table. Barbie was already sitting on one, distracted by her thoughts it seemed as she stared at the carpet and picked at her fingernails. While Jermaine fetched tea, I said, 'I assume you are referring to the murder of Tarquin Trebeck.' I watched to see if Barbie stiffened at the mention of his name, but she didn't.

'Yes,' he replied, then gasped. 'Has someone else been killed? Is that why you needed to confirm which murder I was talking about?'

'No, Shane. At least not to my knowledge. Now, before you give us too much detail. I need to summon Mr Ikari, the deputy captain. He will want to hear what you have to say.'

'Maybe later,' he replied, almost spilling over with excitement. 'I think we should solve this thing first. Wrap it all up and present it to him once we have all the evidence.'

Why was it everyone thought I was a detective? 'Shane, that's not what I do, I'm just...'

'Who did it?' asked Barbie, looking up for the first time since I had sat down as her question cut me off.

'It was Ian Kenyon,' he revealed.

In response to his certainty, I asked, 'What makes you so certain?' Jermaine appeared with a tray laden with fine china and silverware, but the conversation continued as he set out the cups and saucers and began to pour.

'He's been talking about how much he loathes Tarquin ever since the crew got together. I overhear things. No one notices me so they say things they otherwise wouldn't because they think no one is around to hear.' Shane was nodding at me as he spoke, utterly convinced that he had the answers.

'Yes,' I said. 'But what evidence do you have?'

The question made him pause, but not for long. 'I bet we can find the evidence we need in his room. I bet he has the knife he used to cut his throat right there hidden under a drawer or something.' I doubted anyone would be dumb enough to keep a murder weapon when they could just toss it over the side and feel pretty confident it would never be found. Shane had more to say yet, 'I know all the people on the film crew, all the different characters. I can help you prove that Ian did it. He probably laughed as he cut Tarquin's throat.' He said it gleefully, excited at the prospect of bringing a killer to justice.

This time Barbie did react, making a small noise of distress but Shane didn't notice. Instead, he picked up his tea and took a gulp. 'Wow! This coffee is terrible!' he exclaimed putting his cup back on its saucer. 'What do you say then? Shall we catch him together? I can help you because I have the inside knowledge and a special skill for not being noticed by anyone.' Seeing my sceptical look at his claim of a superpower, he added, 'Honestly, I can stand in a room and everyone ignores me as if I were not there. I am basically invisible when I want to be.'

31

I politely refrained from commenting. However, I did say, 'I am not a detective, Shane. It is not my task to investigate what happened to Mr Trebeck. Mr Ikari, the deputy captain, and his security team will take care of it. I will ask him to come here so you can tell him what you know.'

'I think we should look into this as well, Patty,' said Barbie. 'Someone targeted me, don't forget.'

'Someone targeted you?' repeated Jermaine, protective anger instantly present in his voice.

'Did they?' asked Shane. He had an incredulous look on his face. 'Who?'

Jermaine was tiring of Shane's dimness. 'The point would be to work that out, don't you think?'

Whatever we might or might not do next, I was calling Mr Ikari now. If there was evidence to gather, he needed to hear about it as a priority. He could then decide what he was going to do about Ian Kenyon. After what I saw at dinner last night when Tarquin humiliated him, I wasn't shocked to hear that Ian hated him. Would he stoop to murder though? It was a long way to go from wanting someone dead to actually killing them yourself. Someone had done it though. But why? And why go after Barbie? Had the killer thought that Barbie had seen something?

With that thought reverberating in my mind I turned to her. Jermaine was about to serve breakfast to the terrace and was poised with a tray. 'Would you care to move to the terrace, madam?'

'Yes, of course.' I didn't actually want to move to the terrace but Jermaine put in so much effort always that I felt obliged to play along. 'Can you contact Mr Ikari, please. Give him my best and request that he visit as soon as is convenient. Please explain the nature of the invitation.'

The crab eggs Benedict was sumptuous, the hollandaise sauce plentiful and voluminous but it told me a lot about Barbie's state of mind that she not only ate it, something she would not normally entertain because she stuck rigidly to a controlled diet that met her nutritional needs, but also that she didn't comment on the fact that I was eating it. Under any other circumstances, she would unhelpfully point out that it might be tasty, but so is kale.

I let my guests eat, refraining from commenting on Shane's eating habits as he scoffed his plateful almost before Barbie and I could lift our forks. While he looked around for more, I asked Barbie, 'Did you see anything out of the ordinary last night?'

She swallowed what was in her mouth before saying, 'Nothing has been ordinary since we left Los Angeles, but you are asking me if I saw a killer lurking anywhere.'

'I'm asking why you were targeted this morning and whether the killer thinks you saw something. Do you remember seeing anyone last night that you felt was watching you? Did anyone look away suddenly when you locked eyes with them?'

'Why are you asking all these questions?' Shane wanted to know. 'I already told you who it was. We need to have Mr Akido…'

'Mr Ikari,' I corrected him.

'Yeah, that's what I said. We need to have the deputy captain clap Ian Kenyon in irons and stash him below decks until we arrive in Hawaii. What are we waiting for anyway?'

'Patience is required, Shane. If Ian is indeed the killer, I am sure Mr Ikari will be able to prove it. He will be along shortly and then you will have your chance to tell him what you know.' I was trying to keep him calm as he seemed agitated at the lack of action. I wasn't sure what he expected, but I wasn't hoping for anything exciting to happen. I had endured plenty of excitement on this cruise already.

'Yeah,' he said. 'Yeah, sure.' He was twitching his legs beneath the table, causing it to vibrate with his nervous energy. 'You know what we should do? We should disguise ourselves as room service and let ourselves into his room so we can search it.' He was all a-quiver at the prospect.

'What if he hasn't ordered room service?' I asked. 'Room service usually just hands over what they have brought at the door and depart anyway.'

'Oh yeah,' he said, drumming his fingers on his chin as he thought. 'I've got it!' he yelled and slammed the table, making Barbie jump out of her skin. 'We disguise ourselves as the cleaners and go in with one of the laundry carts. We can legitimately stay in the room for ages then and would be expected to look everywhere and touch everything as we clean the room.'

I wanted to present an argument, but his idea actually held some merit. It was still daft though; we were going to wait for Mr Ikari and he would conduct his investigation without me getting involved, getting shot at or getting anywhere near anyone who might try to murder me. 'We'll keep that one on the backburner for now, shall we?' I had to admit that I liked his spirit. He was something of a lame duck, a term I might have applied to myself until recently when I found my energy and spirit after years of hiding it inside an unfulfilling marriage. Maybe Shane just needed a hand to find his.

The deputy captain arrived fifteen minutes later, just when I was emerging from my bedroom once more after retreating there to shower and change. It was a cloudy day and cooler than most since I had come on board. There was threat of a storm on the horizon, so I chose a long-sleeved top I had bought just last week in one of the boutique shops on board. Its thick cotton would keep me warm, but it had three chunky toggles below my chin that could be opened to keep me cool. It had thin horizontal navy blue and white stripes and went well with the white jeans I had bought at the same time. I thought my look had a pleasing nautical theme to it. Jermaine had helped me pick the items out along with many others from an array of shops, the task necessary because I had dropped a dress size during my time on board, nearly two in fact even though it wasn't an intentional move.

I was glad of the new clothes though, they felt expensive (because they jolly well were!) and made me feel like I fitted in a little better. In the Marks & Spencer's wardrobe I brought on board with me, there had always been a little voice telling me I looked dowdy. Now, I looked elegant and well-groomed.

Jermaine coughed politely as I came into the room, all eyes swinging toward me. He was making his eyes bug out and trying silently to shoo me back into my bedroom with them from across the suite's main living area.

No one else said anything, but Barbie carefully pointed a finger without moving the rest of her hand. I followed the finger down to my legs where I found a pair of knickers stuck to the back of my left leg. They were bright red and now so was my face.

Mr Ikari and his lieutenants were good enough to have looked away and pretend they hadn't seen anything, but Shane was staring open-mouthed and about ready to laugh when Jermaine positioned a single finger under his jaw and pushed it shut.

Mortified, I retreated back into my bedroom, yanked the treacherous underwear from their hiding place and threw them on the bed. Checking myself for any further wardrobe malfunctions, I saw that my hair, which I had elected to leave to air dry and deal with later when I heard Mr Ikari arrive, was beginning to frizz already. So, I plonked myself down at my dressing table and dealt with that too.

By the time I emerged, finally ready to face the day and devoid of extra underwear, Mr Ikari was wrapping up. Was he really done so soon?

As the eyes of the men in uniform swung my way, I said, 'Good morning, gentlemen. Leaving so soon?'

I got three good mornings in return, Mr Ikari continuing to say, 'We have taken a statement from Mr Sussmann.'

'They don't believe me,' snapped Shane, clearly angry.

'That is not accurate.' Mr Ikari's response was delivered in his usual calm tone which seemed to incense Shane further.

'I'm telling you; he did it!' he roared, this time getting to his feet. 'He has wanted him dead for years. He is in his cabin right now, laughing about how he has you all fooled.'

'Mr Kenyon has an alibi for the whole of last night,' replied Mr Ikari, his comment aimed at me though, not at Shane who did not seem inclined to listen. 'So, does everyone else on the film crew that we have spoken to thus far. It would seem that the picture suffered something of a setback last night when Mr Kenyon quit. He sent his resignation to Paul Deacon and cc'd every single member of the film crew, stating that he refused to

36

work with Tarquin Trebeck and that the picture was on hold until he was replaced. I must admit that I do not fully understand the dynamics, but it would appear that the movie cannot continue without a producer.'

'Surely, he was being ridiculous.' I frowned as I tried to understand his demand. 'Wouldn't they let Ian walk first? How can there be a movie if they sack the star of the franchise?'

'Exactly!' said Shane, in a sing-song voice as if we had just made his point for him. 'Ian would have known that there was no way Tarquin would get his come-uppance, so he killed him instead.'

'Nevertheless,' said Mr Ikari without bothering to glance at Shane, 'Mr Kenyon has an alibi for last night and has been dismissed as a suspect from my investigation. I do need to discuss your movements last night though, Mr Sussmann. Can you account for your whereabouts between ten o'clock last night and three o'clock this morning?'

'I was at a party,' Shane replied grumpily. 'Like many of the unimportant members of the film crew, we were not invited to have dinner with the stars.' He shot a glance at Barbie as he said it. 'So, we all threw a big party for ourselves, went to a bar, I forget which one, and when it shut at midnight, we went back to our cabins, opened all the doors and had a party below decks.'

'Can anyone corroborate this?' Mr Ikari asked, making notes in a small notebook.

'Can anyone... you mean, do I have an alibi?' Shane sounded outraged. 'Why on earth would I need one? I'm not the killer, Ian Kenyon is!'

'Do you have someone that can corroborate your whereabouts last night,' asked Mr Ikari again, his calm demeanour stoking Shane's anger.

I saw him open his mouth and close it again. Realising he was about to shout and sensing the futility of doing so, Shane forced his anger back down. 'Mark. Talk to Mark Carling. I was in his room. He gave me a beer to drink.'

'Mark Carling,' echoed Mr Ikari as he jotted the name in his notebook. 'Very good. Thank you, Mr Sussmann.'

'Are you going to question Ian Kenyon again?' Shane asked.

'I have already explained that he has been questioned and dismissed. He has an alibi. I am quite certain he did not murder Tarquin Trebeck last night.'

'But he did!' shouted Shane, his voice rising again as the supressed anger resurfaced. Jermaine moved to position himself behind Shane's chair; ready to act if the smaller man decided to do something rash. 'His alibi is lying. Who is it? Tell me who his alibi is.' When Mr Ikari did not respond to his demands, Shane faked a laugh and filled it with mocking derision. 'You can't, can you? You can't tell me the name of his alibi because he doesn't have one. Don't worry, Mr Ikari, Mrs Fisher and I will solve this case for you and save you from your incompetence.'

I shook my head at Mr Ikari, conveying that I had no intention of doing any such thing. 'I have matters to attend to,' he said, taking his hat from beneath his left arm as a cue to his lieutenants that they were leaving. 'Good day, Mrs Fisher.'

Jermaine had seen their cue and was already at the door to show them out when they got there. As he closed it, Shane jumped to his feet. 'So, what's our next move? Do we go with the maid plan and search his room?'

As gently as I could, I said, 'Shane, we are not going to investigate. I am not a detective. My friend,' I indicated Barbie, 'is quite upset about Tarquin's death, so I think we will spend the day in quiet reflection. Mr Ikari appears to have matters well in hand.'

Quietly, his voice almost a snivel, Shane said, 'But he thinks Ian is innocent.'

'Then he probably is,' I replied, my voice soft and caring. 'Shane, has Ian done something to you in the past? Is there a reason you want him to be the killer?'

'What? No! Why ever would you ask such a thing?' Shane was on his feet and Jermaine was watching him carefully, positioned, once again, just a few feet behind him so he could react if he felt he needed to. Shane was no threat to me though; he was leaving. 'I can see that I have intruded, Mrs Fisher,' he said, his voice returning to a calm level. 'I will gather the evidence I need by conducting my own investigation and will return once I have it.' He went to the door, Jermaine moving ahead of him to open it. At the threshold, Shane turned, bowed flamboyantly and declared, 'I'll be back.' It was a poor attempt at an Austrian accent, but he shot me a smile as he disappeared from my sight.

'Do you think he will do something silly?' asked Barbie. It was the first time she had spoken in a while and her movements in the last hour had been robotic so the fact that she was aware of what was going on came as a relief.

Considering the question, I had to arrive at the conclusion that he very well might do something rash or ridiculous. When I said that, she asked, 'Do you think we should go after him?'

I groaned, wordlessly acknowledging that Barbie probably had a point.

39

'Do you know where his cabin is?' I asked as I looked about for my shoes.

'Not precisely. Most of the extras, cameramen, gaffers, effects and makeup were given cabins on the twelfth deck. Tarquin, Bhavana, Paul Deacon and a few others have suites on the next deck down. They will be easy enough to find, but all of the film crew were booked in as a lump, so the Aurelia's guest management system doesn't say who is in which cabin.'

Barbie lifted herself off the couch in one fluid motion. She was so graceful and balletic that she made it look as if she had done nothing more than send a mental instruction to her perfect abs and they had propelled her from sitting to standing. When I got up, I had to shuffle forward a little, then rock forward so my bodyweight's inertia assisted in getting me onto my feet.

Then, because she had been sitting for a while, Barbie stretched in place, lifting her long graceful arms above her head and holding that pose, then forcing them behind her back so her boobs stuck out. After that she folded neatly at the waist, as if she had no bones, to place her forehead against her shins.

Jermaine saw what we were doing, crossed the room to fetch my bag, and handed Barbie her phone. 'I shall accompany you, madam,' he announced. 'Just in case Mr Sussmann does anything... foolish and my assistance is required.'

I replied with, 'Very good, Jermaine.' I was sure his assistance would not be required but I also believed that he spent too long trapped in my suite doing butler work; he was welcome to escape for a while. He hurried the tray of crockery and silverware back to the kitchen, checked his uniform in the mirror and made his way to the door where I was patiently waiting. I could open the door myself of course, but Jermaine tended to get snippy if he found me doing too much for myself.

Barbie had a general idea where we could find the film crew which was good enough as a starting direction and we could ask for Shane's cabin when we got there. However, it seemed prudent to scope out the suites on the next deck just in case he had gone directly there to bother Ian Kenyon. Unfortunately, the Aurelia is so vast that not knowing the exact number and location of a person's cabin, leaves you staring at a seemingly endless line of closed doors. That didn't happen to us though, as no sooner had we descended one deck and left the stairwell, than we came across an open door with white uniforms of the ship's security visible both inside and out.

One of the men said, 'Good morning, Mrs Fisher.' It was Lieutenant Schneider, a man I had spent some time with recently when he was assigned to protect me from a potential threat.

'Good morning, Stefan,' I replied as he greeted Barbie and Jermaine. To his left was another man, a younger man that looked barely out of his teens and barely able to fill his uniform. He looked so young I had to wonder what the minimum age was for employment in the security team. I didn't say anything, of course, though I doubted he would have heard me if I had; his expression was frozen, his eyes transfixed by my Lycra-clad, perfect, blonde friend, Barbie.

She hadn't noticed, but then Barbie was used to being stared at. The young man's look was not a lecherous one, he was not staring at her chest and grinning, no, he was gawping open mouthed at all of her, drinking her in as if he had just tasted fine wine for the first time and couldn't believe anything could be that good. He had a teenager's crush and he had it bad.

'Is this Tarquin's suite?' I asked. I felt certain that it was and could hear voices coming back through the open door even though I could not see them.

Stefan replied with, 'Yes, Mrs Fisher. You should go in; the captain and Mr Ikari are both in there.'

'Thank you, Stefan,' I smiled in return. This was just what I wanted. But I turned to Barbie. 'Barbie, do you want to wait out here?' I wasn't sure how she felt about going into the suite. She had probably been hoping to spend time in here with Tarquin.

'You can stay out here with us, miss,' said the young guard looking hopeful.

Barbie strode forward though. A determined look fixed to her face as she said, 'I need to face it now. It will just haunt me otherwise.' Stefan stepped aside to let her pass, Jermaine and I following closely behind.

Inside the suite, a small lobby area led through another door to the left and into a living area much like in my suite only smaller. The captain and Mr Ikari were the first two people I saw. They were in the middle of the room going through letters laid out on a table.

'Good morning, Mrs Fisher,' said the captain with a pleasant smile. 'This area is out of bounds for guests at this time, but since it is you…'

I greeted him in return, bidding a good morning to Mr Ikari and everyone else at the same time. 'I'm not here for any particular reason,' I explained. 'We were looking for Ian Kenyon's suite but stumbled upon the guards outside.'

'Well, as you can see, Mrs Fisher, Mr Ikari has his team organised and they are conducting their investigation so please do not touch anything. I merely dropped by myself to check he had sufficient manpower.' He would never openly admit it if he had been checking up on his deputy, but I wondered if perhaps the real reason had been to see if Mr Ikari had any idea what he was doing since his predecessor had proven to be quite incapable.

'Is there any indication as to who might have been the killer?' I asked.

It was the captain that replied though. 'Mrs Fisher, you are not conducting your own investigation, are you?' he asked, frowning.

'No, no,' I blushed. 'No, of course not. I was looking for one of the film crew and he mentioned that he might visit with Ian.'

'Good,' he said with clear relief. 'I wouldn't want to find you in hot water again.'

'I have a book to read, actually. It's a romance novel. I um...' I realised I was rambling and closed my lips.

'To answer your question, Mrs Fisher, it is too early to tell,' said Mr Ikari, diplomatically giving nothing away. It was wise of him to stay tight-lipped. I shouldn't have asked; there was no reason to share information with me.

Suddenly, I got a sense that I was intruding. 'Well, I think we should be on our way,' I said to Jermaine and Barbie as I began moving back toward the door. Then I spotted a poster on the wall. It was faded and a little crumpled but held flat inside a giant frame. It was a movie poster from the late nineties, and I recognised the film but not its significance until I looked closer. 'Is that Tarquin?' I asked, peering at one of the characters displayed.

Her voice quiet and soft, Barbie said, 'Yes, *Summer Adventure* was his first film.'

The title of the film was displayed in bold letters above the gang of boys and girls taking centre stage. Right in the middle was the star of the film, but I didn't recognise him. Perhaps, like so many child actors, he faded into obscurity before he made adulthood. I remembered the film though I couldn't imagine why I would have watched it. It was a tale of discovering sexuality as the young teens battled with puberty and all the drama it brought. Tarquin was a minor actor playing the role of younger brother to the lead in the middle. He appeared on the far left of the arrowhead the children formed.

'Did any of the other children go on to have careers?' I asked.

'I don't know,' Barbie answered. 'But I don't recognise any of their names.'

Jermaine pointed to the child in the middle. 'Whatever happened to the kid that played the lead?' Then he read the name from the poster, 'Jeremiah Anthony Bumblethorpe. Such an unusual name.'

'Yes,' I agreed. 'I would certainly recognise it if he was doing anything today.'

The captain joined us, coming to stand close to me; inside my personal space in fact but I didn't feel uncomfortable with him so close, and acknowledged silently to myself that I liked it. He leaned forward to gaze at the poster, putting his face quite close to mine as he did so. 'It has always struck me as strange that some child actors succeed where others fail.' He raised his eyebrows, keeping any further thoughts on the matter silent. Then he straightened again, saying, 'If you will excuse me, please. Good day, Mrs Fisher.' As the captain swept from the room with a curt nod to everyone else, I felt a slight flutter of disappointment, but in noticing it, I squashed it flat. I had no time nor need for a man, even one as handsome and accomplished as Captain Alistair Huntley. I was still married, though it had been more than a week since I last spoke to my husband. Sooner or later I would have to make a decision about our future.

'We should go,' I said, snapping myself out of a daydream. 'Mr Ikari, do you know where Ian Kenyon's suite is?' I asked as I walked toward the door.

'Two doors along toward the stern,' he replied without looking up. I guess he had been there already as part of his investigation.

Ian Kenyon wasn't in though. We knocked and waited but there was no sound from within. A fleeting concern that Shane was inside the suite already made my adrenalin spike for a heartbeat, but I dismissed the notion. Shane was excitable and enthusiastic, but I didn't think he would actually do anything.

'To the twelfth deck then?' asked Barbie. 'We might as well see if we can find Shane while we are already out and about,' she said brightly. I didn't argue with her. Though I had no need to find Shane; I wasn't concerned that he was going to do anything foolish and I had assured the captain I was not poking my nose into Mr Ikari's investigation, I was concerned that Barbie was using the search for Shane to distract herself from Tarquin's death and I would play along for as long as she needed.

On deck twelve, the film crew were easy to find because they were coming our way when we got there.

'Hi, Barbie,' said one of a pair of pretty young women as they passed us heading in the other direction.

'Have you seen Shane?' she called after them, but they were already gone. We turned the next corner to find several more people that Barbie recognised. 'Hey, Mark, guys,' she said to the mixed gender group. 'Have any of you seen Shane?'

Mark, the young man in the lead scrunched his face in confusion. 'Shane who?' he asked. 'We're heading up to the wave pool and terrace on deck eighteen if you want to join us. We're all expenses paid, baby, yeah! The star gets himself killed and we get a free holiday.' One of the men just behind Mark, kicked him hard in his ankle. 'Ow, man. What the hell?'

'Shane Sussmann,' Barbie added for clarity, speaking loudly to get Mark's attention back to the subject. She didn't want him to realise his faux pas and make a thing of it. 'About five and a half feet tall, big bushy beard.' She was gesticulating to add emphasis but the sea of faces looking back at her were utterly lost. 'Not ringing any bells?'

Mark turned to face some of his friends as they began exchanging shrugs and questions. He turned back to face Barbie. 'A beard, you say?'

'Yes. He's works in the pyrotechnics department under Carter.' Barbie seemed exasperated. 'You're his friends, aren't you? He said he was at a party in your cabin last night, Mark. He gave your name as his alibi.'

47

Mark flapped his lips a couple of times, trying to find a connection in his head. 'I think I know who you mean, but I haven't seen him recently. He might have been here last night, but I don't remember.'

'Okay, thanks,' Barbie muttered as Mark and his friends started moving again. They were dressed for a day by the pool, probably an unexpected bonus now that the film was in limbo. As they disappeared around the corner behind us, I heard Mark getting berated by his friends for his insensitivity.

Barbie knocked on an open door, finding one of the make-up girls inside. The girl said, 'Oh, hey, Barbie.' When she saw who it was. 'I'm really sorry about Tarquin. Did, you two guys... um, did you...'

'No,' said Barbie. 'No, it wasn't like that. I mean, it might have been, but we'll never know now. I'm looking for Shane Sussmann,' she added, moving the conversation on quickly to avoid discussing Tarquin or her feelings.

'Shane Sussmann?' the young woman replied slowly. 'I don't think I know a Shane Sussmann.'

This was getting weird; no one seemed to know him. Barbie thanked the girl and tried the next door. We got the same result but the passageway and all the rooms that belonged to the film crew were emptying out as the unexpected time off was being put to good use and no one wanted to miss out on the free booze, food and pool time now on offer.

Just as we were about to call it quits, Shane appeared behind us. 'Hey, guys, who are you looking for?' he asked. He was munching a candy bar and had bits of chocolate caught in his beard. He saw the three of us staring at him, became self-conscious of the snack in his mouth and swallowed slowly. 'You want some?' he asked.

Ignoring his question, I said, 'We came looking for you. I wanted to make sure you weren't trying to do anything rash.'

'Like find the proof I need to get Ian Kenyon convicted of Tarquin's murder, you mean?' he locked eyes with me and paused, daring me to claim that he had it all wrong. When I said nothing, he shrugged. 'I decided not to bother.'

'Oh.' I hadn't expected that answer. 'Shane, about your alibi for last night. We were asking people where we could find you and none of them seemed to know who you were and Mark Carling, the man whose cabin you said you were in, he didn't remember you at all.'

Shane was looking at the floor. 'Yeah, well,' he said without looking up. 'I'm forgettable, aren't I? I told you that earlier. People don't really notice me. I was in Mark's cabin for hours last night, I even talked to one of the make-up girls for a while. I thought she might be interested in me since she hadn't tried to move away until I realised she had gone to sleep. I'm not surprised they don't remember seeing me.' He looked up finally, his eyes not quite brimming with tears, but the suggestion that he wanted to cry was there. 'Life would be very different if I was handsome.' I couldn't help feeling sorry for the poor boy. Whatever must it be like to move amongst your fellow humans and never be noticed, never be remembered?

Suddenly he said, 'I should get a tattoo!' His face bore an excited smile. 'Is there a tattoo parlour on board?' the question was aimed at Barbie. 'I bet having a tattoo would make me more memorable. I'll get a giant dragon that starts behind my left ear and sweeps down my neck so that girls can see some of it and want to see the rest. That will give me an excuse to take my shirt off.'

I didn't think taking his shirt off would do him any favours, but I kept quiet.

Barbie's answer took the wind out of his sails anyway. 'Sorry, Shane, there are no tattoo parlours.' Then, as his smile faded, she quickly added, 'There will be plenty in Hawaii though when we come into port. You can spend the time between now and then checking out artwork and working out what you want.' She was selling the idea with a little verve because he seemed so down.

'Yeah. Yeah, that sounds good.' Finally, his mood seemed lifted. He yawned then, opening his mouth wide to show his fillings instead of placing a hand over his mouth. 'If you don't mind, I need to get some sleep. All that partying doesn't agree with me.' I said goodbye but it was to the back of his head as he was already shuffling down the corridor, stopping just two doors further along to fish for his keycard.

'I'm going to go to work, I think,' said Barbie. 'I'm a big ball of energy. I need a spin class or something to distract me. Besides, the others have covered my classes all week while I have been pretending to be an actress; it's time I got back to reality.'

Jermaine and I exchanged a glance but neither of us presented an argument. Maybe burning off some energy and hitting a punchbag would be the most cathartic solution until she felt ready to discuss her feelings. She was already jogging on the spot.

'You go ahead, sweetie,' I suggested. 'Jermaine and I will head back to my suite. I have a book to read.' We air kissed and she left us, heading back to her gym but I would call on her later and maybe see if she wanted to watch a movie or something tonight. She was a big fan of action films, but I would have to pick one that didn't star Tarquin Trebeck.

As she disappeared around the corner ahead of us, Jermaine and I made our way quietly back to my suite. The excitement of the last few days, Barbie's acting, my concern over her relationship with Tarquin all seemed a long way behind me now. Yet again there was an abundance of drama in my life and a mystery I was trying hard to resist.

I read my book as I had intended to, burning through the second half of it and getting toward the end when Jermaine coughed politely to attract my attention. 'Would you care for luncheon, madam?'

His timing was perfect, my stomach had just given a light rumble. 'What do you have in mind?' I asked, always keen to give him the chance to stretch his culinary legs.

'I thought perhaps a smoked salmon souffle with a lime foam and a celeriac slaw.' I could see he was keen to make it and had most likely already gathered the ingredients together.

'That sounds delightful, Jermaine.' It really did. With my mouth starting to salivate at the thought, I closed my book. 'Do I have enough time for a stroll?'

'Of course, madam,' my butler replied as if surprised by the question. 'Luncheon will be served to your timings, madam, not mine.'

'Very good, Jermaine. I shall return in fifteen minutes.' I glanced out of the window to gauge the temperature, and noticed dark clouds forming on the horizon.

Jermaine saw me squinting into the distance. 'There is a storm to the south, madam. Quite a bad one, but the captain will avoid the worst of it. The sun deck might be unpopular for a day or so if we catch the edge of it. Nothing more.'

'I sure hope so,' I murmured to myself as I squeezed a sun hat onto my head to keep my hair in place; it looked breezy. Jermaine went ahead of me to the door as always. Opening it and standing stiffly to the side so I could exit. I had long since given up asking him to relax; he acted as he

52

wanted to act and was happy with it. My resistance to his butlering only seemed to upset him.

Outside, and heading toward the sun terrace, I could see through the panoramic windows that I had underestimated the weather. The pool area, which was usually teeming with sun-worshippers and happy holiday makers, was all but devoid of life. Outside, faint tendrils of moisture were being carried on the air as a cold breeze, the first I had felt since leaving Blighty, sent goosepimples to my skin. The bar was closed for the first-time during daylight hours, making me wonder if Jermaine's prediction of the captain avoiding the storm would prove accurate.

I wanted to leave my suite to stretch my legs and because, if I didn't, I would spend the entire day locked up inside. It wasn't as if it was raining, so I set off around the upper-deck terrace heading for the prow. I loved the view of the endless ocean as it stretched out of sight and fell off the curvature of the earth. There were always dolphins visible too, far below as they danced in the giant vee the ship carved.

Even in the lee behind the bridge, the breeze born by the ship's forward motion was stronger today than usual. The sun decks were shielded from it by design so that almost no wind reached them, but coming around the superstructure to make one's way forward exposed a person to the buffeting it provided. It wasn't strong enough that I needed to hug the side of the ship or lean into it to move forward, but it caused the loose strands of my hair to whip about annoyingly. As I considered turning around, I caught a snippet of conversation on the air.

'...ver get away with it!' It was a man's voice being carried on the breeze. He was shouting and sounded angry. Curious, I pushed onward toward the direction it had to have come from, keeping to the edge of the structure so I might see whoever was there before they saw me.

Then a trill laugh reached my ears. It sounded like Bhavana; I had heard her laugh last night, the sound like someone using a xylophone to imitate trickling water.

A few more steps so I could peek around the leading edge of the mammoth structure the bridge sat above, and I caught sight of the people talking. They weren't talking though, they were arguing. I could see the anger on Ian Kenyon's face. His cheeks were red and his eyes were wide behind his glasses as he poked a finger at the stunning lead actress.

'I would never have believed you could stoop so low,' he said, his voice being carried on the wind to reach me as clearly as if he had been standing next to me.

'Nevertheless,' she replied while grinning triumphantly into his face, 'you cannot now undo what you did last night. The deed is done, and I have the evidence that will destroy you if it gets out.'

'Curse your rotten heart, Bhavana,' he spat.

She laughed again as if the situation was funny. I leaned out a little more. I didn't want them to see me, but Ian had raised his hands as if he was going to attack her. Without taking my eyes off them I fumbled in my bag for my phone. It was a new item, and one that I was still becoming familiar with. Thankfully, when mine went in the pool, we docked a day later and I was able to find a shop to get a new one.

Bhavana's voice carried on the air. 'You will do as I say, Ian, or you can kiss your career, and probably your freedom, goodbye.' My phone was in my hand now but as I brought it up and switched it to the video app, a seagull tried to snatch it from my hands. It was an enormous bird, its flapping wings as wide as my outstretched arms it seemed.

'What was that?' I heard Ian ask, concern obvious in his voice. 'I think there is someone there.'

'I couldn't care if there is, Ian,' laughed Bhavana. 'It changes nothing.'

'Shoo,' I hissed to the bird. My phone went skittering across the deck when the bird made me jump and now it was trying to fight me for the prize. 'It's not food, you stupid bird!' I couldn't shout to scare it off for fear I would be heard, but as I closed my hand around the phone, narrowly avoiding its stabbing beak, I managed to flap my own arm in its face to scare it away. It took off once more, wheeling into the sky with an angry squawk.

'You see?' said Bhavana. 'It's just a bird.'

Slowly, I clambered to my feet, but where Ian had been fifty feet away before, now the distance was less than thirty and he saw me as I stood up. The unexpected closeness made my heart start but thankfully the shot of adrenalin that hit my bloodstream made my feet move too.

I didn't know if he had recognised me, but I wasn't hanging around to find out. I darted back along the side of the ship, keeping close to the curving superstructure leading up to the bridge high above. I could hear that he had caught sight of me when he shouted for me to stop. His cries only made me go faster. I wanted to tell myself that Ian posed no threat to me, but after what I had just heard, I couldn't help but believe Shane might have been onto something.

What evidence did Bhavana have that would destroy Ian? What was it that he couldn't undo from last night? The only conclusion I could form was that Ian was guilty of killing Tarquin and the alibi he provided Mr Ikari was false. If that was true, then would he target me if he thought I had overheard him?

I thought all these things as I ran away, reaching the edge of the superstructure and the sun deck beyond it with no idea how close Ian Kenyon might be. I didn't want to look back to check his proximity because then he would see my face.

I stayed like that, running as fast as I could and not looking back until I was safely inside once more. Turning the final corner to my suite, I grabbed the wall to stop myself and tried to slow my breathing so I could hear if I was still being followed. I had just run more than one hundred yards as fast as I could though, so my pulse was hammering in my ears and my breaths were coming in ragged lumps. The best I could manage was a glance back around the corner, checking my tail in a bid to reassure myself that I was safe now.

'Stop right there!' yelled Ian Kenyon. I wasn't safe! He was twenty yards away, just inside the door to the sun deck and had been standing still while he tried to work out which way I might have gone. Now he was running toward me again and I was fumbling in my bag for my door card as I tried to escape again.

Thankfully, my door was only a few yards away, but I was utterly panicked as I swiped the card at the sensor, shoved the door with my shoulder and tumbled inside.

'Is everything alright, madam?' asked Jermaine. I was on the floor on my entrance lobby with my feet against the door where I had kicked it shut and my butler was standing serenely above me, looking down with a quizzical expression.

I rolled onto my front, accepting Jermaine's hand to regain my feet. 'I was being chased by Ian Kenyon,' I managed between heaving breaths.

Instantly concerned and switching to defensive mode, Jermaine stepped behind me to open the door again.

'Be careful,' I warned. 'I think he really is the killer.'

Snatching the door open, my strong, capable butler stepped forcefully into the corridor, glancing both ways as he flexed his knees and held his hands poised to deal with an attack should there be one. He straightened to his full height after less than a second though, turning to face me as he relaxed. I stuck my head outside; the corridor was empty.

Coming back inside, Jermaine asked, 'Shall I summon Mr Ikari, madam?'

'Yes, I think that would be prudent,' I replied. I was going to make things tough for the deputy captain with the news that I had for him. He had already cleared Ian Kenyon and must therefore have believed his alibi. I wondered who it was.

In the living area of my suite, I could hear Jermaine talking to someone on the ship's phone. My heartbeat was returning to normal and my breathing was back under control, but I was still wearing my jacket and shoes. I took the shoes off in deference to Jermaine's cleaning regime and shucked my jacket because I was warm now, a combination of coming back in out of the cool air outside and the exertion of running had pushed my body temperature up.

Jermaine said, 'Mr Ikari will attend momentarily, madam. Would you care for luncheon while you wait for him?'

Luncheon? Yes, of course. Despite being Jamaican, my butler had a wonderful sense of British reservation. He gave the impression that he would stop for tea at four o'clock even if the ship was on fire or we were being shot at.

He was probably right in that I had time to eat now but once Mr Ikari arrived the opportunity to eat would be lost for some time. Plus, he had made smoked salmon souffles and they would be ruined if not eaten when they were ready.

The food was as wonderful as one might imagine it to be. Light and delicate with a depth of flavour a Michelin starred chef might struggle to achieve. It tasted indulgent but I knew Jermaine was obeying Barbie's nutritional instructions to keep the calorie count low.

The expected knock at my door came just as Jermaine was clearing away my crockery and silverware. The knock came again before he answered the door though, refusing to be rushed as he believed a butler's duties included remaining calm no matter what.

Mr Ikari came into my suite flanked by two of his guards as always, one of them the ultra-young-looking man from earlier. The other was one I had seen but not been introduced to. He bore a bored expression and had the look of a man that had a higher opinion of himself than was warranted.

'Mr Ikari.' I rose from the table and crossed the room to greet him.

'Good afternoon, Mrs Fisher. This is Lieutenant Pippin,' he said, indicating the youthful man in his oversized uniform, 'and Lieutenant Charpentier.' Both men nodded their heads in greeting. 'Special Rating Clarke said you had been chased?'

'Yes, by Ian Kenyon.' I explained what I had seen and overheard, the exchange between Ian and Bhavana one that I felt was quite damning. 'You said that Ian had an alibi, but I have to question who that was and whether they might have been covering for him. Bhavana clearly has evidence from last night that he doesn't want anyone to see or know about.'

Mr Ikari listened patiently, nodding and keeping politely quiet while I explained the events at the prow of the ship. When I finished, he gritted his teeth and sucked in some air. What was he waiting for? He seemed to be deliberating his next move when he ought to be acting upon what I had just told him.

'Might we have a word in private?' he asked. The question surprised me but if he felt he had information to give me that he wanted as few people as possible to hear, then I could offer no argument.

'Of course,' I said and turned to move.

'*We* shall vacate the room, madam,' said Jermaine, turning to the two lieutenants. 'Come along gentlemen. Privacy is at the discretion of the guest.'

'What?' asked Lieutenant Charpentier, his French accent shining through his perfect English.

'This is Mrs Fisher's suite, sir,' replied Jermaine. 'When she calls for privacy, it is not she that finds somewhere new to go for it.' Jermaine held his arm out to guide the men from the suite and though the guard looked unhappy about the arrangement he kept his lips shut as he filed to the entrance lobby and outside.

When the door shut, Mr Ikari turned to face me and said, 'Mr Kenyon has an alibi that cannot be disputed. It involves another member of the film crew. So, despite what you might have heard, I have evidence that I consider to be indisputable.'

'What evidence?' I asked, seriously curious about why he was being so secretive.

'That, Mrs Fisher, I cannot tell you,' he replied.

I wanted to ask why but the door opened again, Jermaine's apologetic face appearing around the door frame. He said, 'There is an urgent message for Mr Ikari, madam.' He delivered the message to me, but then swung his gaze to the deputy captain.

Mr Ikari waved that Jermaine should come back in. 'Let's hear what he has to say.'

Jermaine was followed into the room by Lieutenants Charpentier and Pippin and Lieutenant Baker, a man I knew well enough to wave and smile at.

'Mrs Fisher,' he said by way of greeting. 'I ran here rather than use the radio, sir,' he said to Mr Ikari. 'One can never tell who might overhear the radio.'

Mr Ikari made a circular motion with his hand, asking him to get on with it. 'Tell us what you have for us, Mr Baker.'

'Yes, sir. There has been another incident at the gym, sir.'

'Is it Barbie?' I pretty much screeched.

With panicked eyes now that I was staring at him, Baker gulped and nodded. 'Yes, ma'am.'

I don't remember telling my feet to move but they were, and Jermaine was ahead of me, like a blocker clearing the field. We were out of the suite's main door, turning left and running along the passageway in the direction of the upper deck gym where Barbie worked. The sound of booted feet behind me told me the ship's security had followed me from my suite and we all arrived at the frosted glass a few seconds later.

Bursting through the door half a pace after Jermaine, I saw four white uniforms milling about and Barbie looking miserable on a chair in the corner. It was the same chair as she had been sitting on when I arrived first thing this morning. Jermaine crossed the room to kneel at her feet and wrap her into a hug.

'Report,' demanded Mr Ikari coming through the door after me.

All the faces in the room turned to look at him but it was Lieutenant Schneider that answered. 'Sir, Miss Berkeley appears to have been threatened.' He pointed to the wall where the photographs of the gym instructors were hung.

It took a second for my eyes to see what he was pointing at, but when I did, my mouth fell open. There were ten, eight inch by ten inch photographs of the gym staff. Each of them showing a smiling face but only one of them had the words, "Your next" daubed on it in in red paint. Even though grammatically incorrect, the message was clear. Someone had defaced Barbie's picture and threatened to kill her. The message had been clear to Barbie as well.

'What do I do, Patty?' asked Barbie, her quiet voice cutting through the silence like a knife.

As the eyes in the room swung to me, I said the only thing I could. 'You move in with me until this is over.'

Barbie stayed where she was, looking miserable and confused for the next fifteen minutes while the security detachment confirmed that no one had seen anything. There were no prints on the picture and no indication as to who might have left the message. It wasn't much of a leap to assume that the message was left by the same person that booby trapped her locker this morning. Barbie was rattled and she was right to be so. She would be safer staying in my suite though, at least that was what I believed. Jermaine could protect her from anyone that intended her harm and I was prepared to believe that if anyone was planning to hurt her, they would not be able to find her if she stayed away from her cabin and the gym.

Mr Ikari came to my side, facing away from everyone else and speaking quietly so they couldn't hear. 'Mrs Fisher, if you want to host Miss Berkeley in your accommodation, I will not attempt to stop you, but I must insist that I post two guards with you.'

I sighed internally. It wasn't the first time I would have guards in my suite but at least this time they would be there to protect someone, not stop me from leaving.

'Have you any idea who is behind this?' I asked, my voice just as hushed as his had been.

I felt him grimace as much as saw it. 'Not yet, Mrs Fisher, but it seems likely that the person that killed Tarquin Trebeck is the same person now targeting Miss Berkeley. One can only imagine their motive.'

I agreed. I had no idea why anyone would target Barbie; she is such a sweet girl. I glanced at the message cruelly written on her picture again. I couldn't let anything happen to her, but I also felt confident that no killer, no matter how motivated, would attempt to get to her if she was securely squirreled away in the confines of my cabin with two guards plus Jermaine to protect her. The woman in question hadn't moved from her seat since we arrived. She was withdrawn and hugging herself for comfort.

'Have you further need for Barbie?' I asked Mr Ikari.

The neat Japanese man looked at her, looked at the defaced picture and slowly shook his head. 'No, Mrs Fisher. If you are ready to go…'

I held out my hand for Barbie to take and Jermaine helped her to her feet. I wondered if she might wobble but, though she looked a little lost, she was able to walk.

'Charpentier, Pippin, you will accompany Mrs Fisher to her cabin and act as personal guard to Miss Berkeley. She goes nowhere without you, though it will be safest if she goes nowhere at all until we have the killer in custody.

'How long will that take?' asked Lieutenant Charpentier, his delicious French accent doing nothing to hide his disdain.

Mr Ikari eyed him carefully, the man was bordering on being insubordinate. 'Baker, you go with them and stay with Miss Berkeley while the other two fetch personal effects from their accommodation.' Mr Ikari was acknowledging that it might be days before the killer was caught. They appeared to have little to go on at this time so Pippin and Charpentier would need spare uniform, underwear, wash gear etcetera.

The men replied with a, 'Yes, sir,' though it was far less enthusiastic from Lieutenant Charpentier. With Jermaine leading the way and Barbie holding my arm, we made our way back to my suite.

The afternoon had barely begun when we arrived in my suite, but most of the next hour was taken up by Barbie, Pippin and Charpentier collecting their gear and moving in.

'I will collect your items for you, Miss Berkeley,' offered Lieutenant Baker. 'Far better that I take a list and go than you expose yourself to further risk by going yourself.'

'No, I really ought to go,' replied Barbie. 'There isn't much that I need and very little danger that the killer will have been able to booby trap my cabin.'

Baker didn't wish to be swayed. He was trying to do his job and keep her safe. 'If there isn't much that you need, could you perhaps do without it? Mr Ikari will be working hard to uncover the killer's identity, perhaps you will not be staying in Mrs Fisher's suite for long.'

'It really needs to be me that goes,' she insisted. 'I don't want you, or anyone else, riffling through my underwear drawer, thank you very much.'

Baker bowed his head as he said, 'I can assure you complete discretion, Miss Berkeley. I can collect the items you request and return here without need to go where I ought not to. Perhaps you have a girlfriend below decks that you can appoint to watch me.'

'Very good,' replied Barbie, folding her arms and squinting her eyes. 'I need a fresh supply of tampons, the medium flow ones, not the heavy flow, I am a couple of days in now, and I want my time of the month panties, please. I keep them in the same drawer as my regular panties, but they are...'

Baker held up a hand in surrender, his cheeks colouring already. 'Perhaps two of us can accompany you to collect your necessaries.'

Barbie said, 'I think that would be best.' Then quickly air-kissed both me and Jermaine before heading off to fetch what she needed. All three guards went with her, there being no need to leave one with me.

'Do you believe it could be Ian Kenyon?' asked Jermaine once we were alone. He had a vested interest in finding out who was after his friend. He and Barbie were very good friends and he possessed a natural protective instinct.

'I want to say yes, but Mr Ikari assures me that it cannot be him. He used the term indisputable evidence but didn't elaborate on what that means.' What I overheard at the ship's prow still bothered me, as did the fact that Ian Kenyon gave chase. I kept reminding myself that I was not a detective and that I had no business involving myself in Mr Ikari's investigation. Furthermore, I promised the captain I wouldn't, but niggling thoughts kept creeping into my head.

Part of me wanted to call on Ian Kenyon so I could quiz him myself, but I knew I wouldn't do it. It wasn't in my nature. I was confident that Mr Ikari would through tenacity and intellect, track down the killer responsible for murdering Tarquin and for threatening Barbie. So, with nothing better to do and the weather continuing to deteriorate outside, I settled once more into an armchair and picked up my book to finish.

Some thirty minutes later, when I had a scant twenty pages left to read and the big climax of the story was reaching its crescendo, a knock at the door preceded Barbie and her two guards returning. Baker had left them at the door, satisfied that he had done his job. I was so drawn into my book that I had utterly forgotten they were even coming back.

Barbie had a light bag slung over one shoulder, but the two men were carting enough gear to last them a month. 'What is all that?' I asked, worried that they were moving in for good.

'Just our uniforms and spare gear,' said Pippin, his cheeks colouring as if he had been caught doing something naughty.

'Really? All that?'

This time it was Charpentier that answered. 'Well, you see, we have our standard number two dress uniform, otherwise known as whites which you are used to seeing us in. But it can be quite hot to wear so we have a separate tunic beneath it which most of us change twice a day just because it keeps us hygienic, not all of us though, eh, Pippin. Some of us haven't quite filled our uniforms yet so have a bit more breathing space for air to circulate.' Pippin just smiled in an embarrassed way rather than argue with the older man. 'Then there's number eight dress which we are permitted to wear if we are above decks in the sun. It is a reduced version of number four dress which was faded out a few years ago and comes with the option of shorts or long trousers depending on the captain's orders. All of these dress uniforms come with a choice of shoes depending on the weather and it is the crew person's responsibility to ensure they have all of the options to hand and ready to wear at all times. Isn't that right, Pippin.'

Pippin nodded vigorously.

'Of course, I was French Foreign Legion before I got injured and had to join this untidy rabble. Now they were a unit that knew how to dress.' Charpentier had humped his gear into one of the bedrooms as indicated by Jermaine. Pippin went into another and Barbie yet another. There were more than enough bedrooms to go around and all of them had their own attached bathrooms and palatial fittings. My suite suddenly felt quite crowded and I hoped Mr Ikari would call soon to say they had found the smoking gun, so to speak.

Barbie re-emerged from her bedroom, her hair pulled into a neat ponytail and a zip-through hoody over the top of her Lycra for the first time ever. 'It's so much cooler today,' she commented. 'I never expect the cool air on this leg, but this far out in the Pacific I ought to not be surprised. Do you think the storm will catch up to us?' she asked.

The question had probably been aimed at me, but it was Charpentier who answered, his voice echoing out from his bedroom. 'Very likely, Miss Berkeley. There will be no cause for alarm though. Charpentier will be here to protect you.'

'From a storm?' she asked, a mocking tone in her voice. 'How exactly will you manage that?' Charpentier was trying to impress her. Talking and acting tough because he was the larger man of the pair, not hard when compared with Pippin but he chose that moment to walk out of his bedroom in his sleeveless tunic. It did a good job of showing off his muscular arms, but I doubted Barbie was impressed by them; she saw bigger arms on her fellow gym instructors every day.

'From anything,' he replied. 'You will be quite safe so long as I am by your side. You should stay as close to me as possible.'

Barbie rolled her eyes at me, then shot a wicked grin in my direction – she was going to do something naughty. 'Would you like that?' she asked him, waiting for him to raise an eyebrow in question. 'If I stayed close to you?' He was only a couple of paces from her, but she closed the distance to him anyway, stepping inside his personal space and tilting her neck to look up at him. His grin turned lecherous as he eyed her up and he opened his mouth to speak, but Barbie cut him off when she curled her lip and sniffed deeply. 'You smell, Lieutenant Charpentier. I suggest you get a shower if you even want to be in the same room as me.'

I tried to hide my smirk as she opened the trapdoor, but I could see that he had spotted it, his cheeks beginning to glow as Barbie turned away from him and went to see what Pippin was doing. Behind her, Charpentier's bedroom door shut.

Jermaine moved behind me, speaking quietly by my ear as he did, 'That ought to keep him quiet for a while.' I couldn't tell if Charpentier was a capable man or not. Perhaps he had been in the French Foreign Legion and had fought battles and perhaps he hadn't, but Jermaine was a study in contrasting styles. I knew he was capable and dangerous, but he would never speak of it and remained modest at all times.

It was mid-afternoon, which meant Jermaine was beginning to prepare tea to be served at four o'clock. Barbie wanted to help out, Jermaine letting her because he recognised her need for distraction, but it was odd to see him let someone inside his inner sanctum. The kitchen was his domain, but he surprised me by then inviting Pippin to join in too. He was making macaroons; delicate little cakes sandwiched together with a creamy filling and taking the time to teach his two students.

I stayed out of the way and stayed quietly reading while, for the first time during my trip, rain beat against the windows. The captain's best efforts to avoid the storm might be keeping us from the worst of it, but it was decidedly inclement outside which made staying inside more bearable. Jermaine and his two budding sous chefs seem to enjoy themselves, laughing and joking. They even invited Charpentier to join them when he finally re-emerged from his room after almost an hour of sulking. He declined though, choosing instead to cross the room and stare out at the storm outside.

When I said nothing, and continued reading my book, a murder mystery this time, he started talking to me anyway. 'This is nothing, you know?' he said, waiting until I looked up before indicating out of the window to the storm. 'Yeah, I got caught in a really bad one with the boys a few years back. We had just finished an operation… I can't tell you where, but let's just say it made the papers the next day. Well, anyway, we were taking a launch back to the drop-off ship when a storm blew in. The waves had to be a hundred feet tall or more. That was a real storm.'

I blinked at him, wondering if he really expected me to have a response to his wild story. Thankfully, he decided he was bored and wandered across to the TV to find an action movie in the ship's extensive built in library. It was something with Jason Statham kicking people, though the director appeared to have saved money on story writers by not bothering to include one. I stayed where I was and did my best to ignore him.

Promptly at four o'clock, Jermaine rang a little bell, I had no idea where he had got it from, but it vanished into one of his suit's pockets once he had our attention. 'Tea is served,' he announced.

'They had the worst food in the legion,' announced Charpentier, making sure any conversation was about him. 'They did it to prepare us of course, make it so we could live on almost anything.'

Barbie poured herself a cup of tea and added skimmed milk but frowned in confusion about his latest statement. 'But you were saying earlier about how they made you do so much exercise.'

'Yeah, that's right. Got to make the men strong,' he answered while pumping both his biceps to show them off.

'Well, the equation doesn't balance,' she argued, selecting several egg sandwiches. 'I'm carb loading right now because I plan to exercise in an

69

hour. The legion would have had to give you enough calories and a balanced nutrition regime in order to make their soldiers strong. Too many calories out through hard exercise and too few calories in through poor diet and the body burns the muscles off first, retaining the body fat as a fuel source because it senses the equation isn't balanced.'

She hadn't bothered to look up while she was speaking, she had been stirring her tea and looking about at the selection of food instead but looked up now to see that Charpentier was once again lost for words.

The pattern continued throughout the evening. Charpentier would strike up a story about himself, regale us with an anecdote about how he had done something heroic or tough and Barbie would generally shoot him down. It made little difference though, as if the only topic of interest to Lieutenant Charpentier was Lieutenant Charpentier.

I elected to get an early night and left the room as he was telling Pippin how the scene on the television was completely unrealistic. An actor, in whatever film they were watching had trodden on a landmine. Charpentier was explaining the top ten ways the actor could extricate himself, but they all sounded like utter nonsense.

Barbie had already retired, her bedtime usually far earlier than mine as she was always up so early to open the gym. It had been a tough day for the poor girl, but the afternoon and evening had passed without incident or alarm. I hoped she would sleep and as I drifted off, my thoughts were all about Ian Kenyon and Tarquin Trebeck. There was a killer on board and whoever it was still had at least one victim planned. I wasn't going to let them get Barbie though, but as sleep took me, I couldn't help but observe that it would be much easier to stop them if I knew who they were.

I awoke early as was my habit but the sun, which had been beating against my curtains every morning since I came on board, was strangely absent this morning. The room was far darker than I was used to, and I almost turned over and went back to sleep assuming, in my sleep-addled state, that it was the middle of the night. Muscle memory made me look at the clock, my eyes closing again and my head settling into the pillow before the message regarding the time caught up with me.

What would Barbie be doing right now? I knew she was an early riser, getting up to be the first in the gym and going to bed early to ensure she achieved her allotted amount of sleep. The answer, I discovered upon leaving my bedroom, was teaching a class in my living area.

As usual, she was clad head to toe in tight lycra, the material showing every curve, which was fine if, like Barbie, you had no body fat, but on me, I suspected I would look like a colourful baked potato. I had no intention of finding out.

Her student was the young and utterly besotted Lieutenant Anders Pippin. He had on a pair of shorts that were probably not supposed to be baggy, but on his matchstick-like legs they floated about like the end of a wizard's sleeve.

I recognised the form of exercise to be High Intensity Interval Training (HIIT), a generally short workout that can be completed using only body weight by attacking an exercise for a block of time, then resting briefly and starting again on the next exercise. The one thing I knew about HIIT was that I didn't like it. It got you out of breath and kept you that way. I tried it a couple of times under Barbie's guidance, but it reduced me to a quivering, sweat-soaked mess in no time at all. I liked longer, more evenly paced exercises.

'And squats,' instructed Barbie, dropping vertically down until her perfect buttocks almost touched the floor then back up again and kept repeating the motion with Anders standing opposite her and straining his neck to not look at her erect nipples poking through the fibre of her top.

I skirted around them as I crossed the room, heading for the freshly brewed coffee Jermaine had already set out. 'Morning, Patty,' called Barbie without breaking stride. 'And rest,' she said.

'Morning, Mrs Fisher,' said Anders between panting breaths. The top half of his cotton tee-shirt was drenched with sweat and he looked about ready to collapse.

'Jermaine stepped out, Patty,' said Barbie as she took a sip of water. 'He said you asked him to make something called a full English and he wanted fresh provisions for breakfast.'

I grabbed the coffee pot and poured a cup of steaming black liquid, the scent of it zipping messages to my brain, telling me it was breakfast time and there should be bacon to go with the coffee. In the weeks that I had been on board the Aurelia, I had lost a dress size and was close to losing a second. Partly that was because I had started out with an idea that I wanted to lose weight, but when I questioned my motivation to do so and realised I was trying to do it for a cheating husband, I changed tack and went in a different direction. Ironically, the different direction was to make myself stronger. I was doing it for myself now, pushing my boundaries and making myself mentally and physically tougher. The weight loss came as a side effect. The full English breakfast though was something I had been craving for quite a while. Before the cheating, before my life changed and I became the lady in the Windsor Suite, I would eat a full English breakfast on a regular basis. Sausage, bacon, eggs, beans, grilled tomato, fried bread, mushrooms, hash browns, and, if I could get it, black pudding. Jermaine had been enthused at the idea, so I was excited that he was currently out getting ingredients.

Behind me, Barbie interrupted my mental salivation as she called out, 'Burpees.' And the pair of them threw themselves on the floor, bouncing back up again and then throwing themselves down once more.

'What is all this racket?' demanded Lieutenant Charpentier emerging from his bedroom wearing boxer shorts, socks and a vest. With very little clothing on I could see just how muscular he really was. He was also good-looking, but his positive traits ended there because not even his French accent could make up for his obnoxious streak. He giggled when he took in Pippin's sweaty exterior.

I kept quiet though I felt like taking the man to one side for a conversation about his ego. I would call Mr Ikari when the hour was more decent and request that Charpentier be replaced by someone else. He was moving toward the kitchen now, causing me to vacate it lest he attempt to strike up a conversation with me about himself – the only topic that interested him. Moving to the doors that opened to my private sun terrace, I took in the dark sky outside. Rain had been falling but it was currently dry. Curious, I cracked the door to see if it was windy. There was a light breeze, nothing more.

Deciding that the conditions outside were tolerable made me instantly want to get out of my suite. Now I would get to use Charpentier's ego against him. 'Lieutenant Charpentier, are you much of a runner?' I asked, the question set to lead him into a trap.

'Running? I won every race I ever entered,' he boasted predictably. 'I thought about a career in athletics, but I needed more excitement and adventure in my life.'

'Jolly good. Barbie,' I called to get her attention. She was currently performing one leg pistol squats, an exercise I had tried and not mastered, falling on my butt each time I lowered myself because I did not seem to have sufficient leg strength to get back up.

Barbie held up a hand with her index finger aloft; asking for a moment's grace. I waited, sipping my coffee until she had performed another three squats and called a halt to the HIIT session. Poor Pippin smiled with relief when she said it was over, but I hoped he had some energy left for what I was about to propose.

'Barbie, would you like to come for a few laps on the top deck? I need to get some exercise in, but I really want to get some fresh air and I think we should avoid the gym in case the killer targets it again. The two lieutenants can accompany us.' Then, taking in Pippin's flushed cheeks, I added, 'Once Mr Pippin has had a rest and some water, of course.'

Barbie had started doing warm down stretches already, but she smiled at me with excited eyes as she said, 'Getting out for a run sounds wonderful, Patty. We can all go. What's the weather like outside?'

I checked again in case it had changed in the last minute. 'It's dry for now.'

'Super.' She looked at Pippin. 'Are you ready to go, Anders? This will target your cardiovascular endurance, the perfect follow up to the high intensity of the interval training which will have overloaded your muscles.'

'What muscles?' chuckled Charpentier. Pippin's face flushed self-consciously.

Barbie acted as if she hadn't even heard him speak. 'It is important after this much exercise for you to ensure you feed your body correctly,'

74

Barbie explained. 'When we get back, I will talk you through macro-nutrients.'

Ten minutes later, four of us set off for a jog around the upper deck of the ship. Jermaine returned as we were getting ready, electing to stay behind and prepare breakfast while we were out. I had jogged the route we were taking many times before, but today I knew I had a breakfast of champions to come back to and a little voice at the back of my head was telling me I needed to get out and put in some effort to earn it. Life on board a luxury cruise liner could be as relaxing or as energetic as a person chose, I tried to strike a balance but pushed myself to go further and further each time I went for a run as I could feel myself getting fitter. The route around the upper deck was too short, so I always went down one flight of stairs to deck nineteen. There I had a route that had to be at least five hundred yards long.

As we jogged the route around deck nineteen, the guards did not express any concern about the killer lying in wait for Barbie though I saw them both looking around, scanning the way ahead in a cautious manner.

We took five laps before I decided I had run far enough, but Barbie and the chaps kept going as I slowed to a stop near the door that led back to the stairs we had come down. I watched their backs disappear around a corner, heading toward the prow then they were lost to sight though I knew they would appear again from the stern soon enough.

Warm from the exercise, I stayed outside while I reran what I had heard yesterday. If Ian wasn't the killer, then what was it that he had done two nights ago that he wouldn't want anyone to find out about? What was the evidence Bhavana held over him? I fetched up against the railing and stared down into the churning grey depths below. Now that I thought about it, why hadn't the killer simply dumped Tarquin's body over the side? It sounded like the easy way to delay an investigation and remove evidence. How would the body ever be found?

The breeze had dropped to almost nothing, but the sky threatened worse weather to come. As I thought that, the rain started to fall again, fat drops of warm water, slowly at first, but building up. I turned to go inside and saw Barbie, Pippin, and Charpentier heading toward me again. Perhaps their pace had been quickened by the coming rain, or perhaps I had been standing outside longer than I thought but I waved that I was heading inside and went to hold the door for them.

As they neared, a piece of litter skipped across the deck. Caught on the breeze, it fluttered and jumped until it neared the three runners and Barbie stamped a foot to pin it down. Pippin had tried to grab it himself but missed. Only Charpentier paid it no mind, keeping his pace to get in from the rain which was how the table came to hit him on his head and miss the other two.

I jumped out of my skin. One moment the broad shouldered, handsome, but above all, obnoxious and self-centred guard had been running to get inside. The next, he was wearing a table as a hat. It flattened him instantly, the space where he had been now empty to reveal Barbie and Pippin beyond, both looking as stunned as I felt.

One thing was clear: Lieutenant Charpentier wasn't the intended target, Barbie was.

'There's someone up there!' shouted Pippin as he dashed toward a set of outside stairs. Barbie was frozen, as I had been, but I was moving now. The nineteenth deck was wider and longer than the twentieth, much like the tiers on a cake, and the point where we exited the ship was beneath the upper deck sun terrace. All the tables were cleared away to stop the storm winds getting them, so this had to be a deliberate act intended to cause harm.

As I came out from under the overhang, I checked above, worried there might be other objects to follow the table. Charpentier had a head wound that was bleeding onto the deck, bright red blood mixing with the rain. 'Help me get him underneath the canopy,' I yelled at Barbie. She hadn't moved yet, the expression on her shocked face unchanged until I shouted. As she grabbed an arm, still looking like she was in a daze, the two of us dragged him a few feet to safety. Tucked beneath the overhang, no further objects could be thrown onto him from above and he was out of the rain. Barbie still bore a blank expression though. I grabbed her shoulder and shouted in her face, 'Look after him. I'll get help.'

She nodded her head, wordlessly acknowledging that she had a task to do as I clambered to my feet and went after Pippin. I didn't have my phone with me, so I had no way of contacting anyone and the weather had kept everyone inside. Everyone but the killer and his intended victim, that is.

I reached the stairs Pippin had taken, grabbed the railing to swing myself around and ran up them three at a time. Well, I started going up them three at a time, but my legs soon reminded me that not only had a I just run several miles, but I was also overweight, over fifty and out of shape. I got to the top deck though, my legs wobbly by the time I got back on the flat.

77

'Pippin,' I called as loud as I could manage between gasps for air. 'Pippin.' There was no sign of him, or of anyone else. I was on the upper deck sun terrace, not far from the door that led back to my suite. Just then Pippin reappeared. He looked bedraggled, making me wonder what I looked like now. It was inconsequential I decided as I convinced my feet to start running again.

Pippin was moving faster, closing most of the distance as he came to me. 'Whoever it was, they got away,' his voice betraying excitement, frustration and apology. 'There was an old couple though. They said they saw someone, but they wanted to get out of the rain. They went for breakfast in the upper deck restaurant.'

The killer had got away. I should be thankful that Barbie was unharmed but had the killer hung around to see the table miss its target? That was when I saw what I had done and screamed her name, 'Barbie!' She was unguarded and borderline in shock tending the fallen Lieutenant Charpentier. 'We have to get to her,' I yelled, grabbing Pippin's arm as I started running back toward the stairs terrified for what I might find.

Yelling her name all the way, I swung myself off the handrail again and back onto the nineteenth deck to find Barbie just where I had left her, but she wasn't alone.

Ian Kenyon was behind her! She hadn't seen him, her back to the door he had just come out of as she bent over Lieutenant Charpentier.

I yelled, 'Get him!' as I slapped Pippin on the shoulder. His young legs powered him forward, accelerating away from me as he began to yell a banshee war cry. The sound like something primal to reinforce his attack.

Ian Kenyon froze, his mouth forming a surprised O before the young guard barrelled into him, knocking him from his feet. I heard the

Hollywood film producer swear as Pippin tackled him, a string of expletives colouring the air.

Then they were fighting. Pippin trying to grapple for a hold that would let him pin the other man. 'You are under arrest!' I heard him shout, just before Ian Kenyon lined up a fist and punched him hard on the chin.

Barbie was cowering away from them as they rolled about on the wet deck, but she didn't leave the injured man she was protecting. From the deck, Lieutenant Charpentier groaned and opened his eyes. 'You can't arrest people, you muppet. We are ship security, not the police.' He tried to sit up though he soon gave up which I felt was clear indication that he was genuinely in need of medical attention.

'Get off me, you moron,' demanded Ian, once again trying to extricate himself from Pippin's fumbling grip. 'What in earth is going on? Somebody please tell me before I start suing you all.'

Shouting voices from behind me caused me to turn my face in their direction, and there, like heroes emerging from the mist, were Lieutenants Baker and Schneider, two men I wish I had requested as protection for Barbie in the first place.

'He tried to kill Barbie again,' I explained quickly as they reached me. My pointed arm sent them to Pippin and Ian Kenyon who were still tussling on the wet deck. To break them up, Baker grabbed Pippin while Schneider hooked a meaty arm around Ian. They pulled them apart easily, their greater size and strength showing.

'Let go of me, dammit,' insisted Ian but Schneider politely refused.

He said, 'Sir, I am going to have to ask you to calm down.'

'He attacked me!' Ian raged, pointing at Pippin. Pippin had a fat bottom lip that had split and a cut to his left eyebrow, which was also bleeding. Baker had hold of his collar, but the young man recognised that the fight was over and was trying to look dignified and righteous.

Calmly, he extended his arm to gesture toward Ian. 'He dropped a table from the upper deck sun terrace. I believe his intended target was Miss Berkeley, but he missed, the table striking Lieutenant Charpentier instead.'

'I did no such thing, you little twerp. I came outside for a cigarette, since we are not allowed to smoke anywhere inside on this godforsaken barge, not even in our own cabins, and he attacked me.' Ian Kenyon was hoping mad.

'I have a pair of witnesses,' replied Pippin calmly. 'An old couple who were on the upper deck terrace when Mr Kenyon threw the table over the edge. They are taking breakfast in the restaurant right now.'

Baker nodded at Schneider. 'I think we had better call Mr Ikari, get a doctor to look at Charpentier, and have a discussion with the witnesses,' he said.

Ian Kenyon wasn't satisfied with his answer though. 'This is preposterous. I'm not listening to another word of this nonsense. You idiots can do what you want.' He moved to leave, but Schneider still had hold of him. 'Let go man!' Ian all but screamed in the taller man's face.

Schneider looked down at Ian Kenyon and I think he was genuinely trying to not appear threatening when he said, 'I'm afraid I cannot do that, sir. Not until we have this cleared up. I can escort you back to your suite if you wish though.'

Ian continued to struggle though, barking, 'Unhand me, man.' Into Schneider's face, so it brought great relief when more white uniforms could be seen approaching us at a jog. They were inside but visible through the windows. Leading them was Mr Ikari, but he wasn't pleased to see me when he came outside and spotted Mr Kenyon dangling from Schneider's arm.

'That's enough now, Lieutenant Schneider.' Mr Ikari's instruction was delivered in a manner that suggested no discussion would be tolerated and none was ventured. Schneider released Ian Kenyon without a word, the smaller man angrily stepping away to find his own space then yanking his clothes straight again. 'It's about damned time,' he snapped. 'I demand to know what is going on.'

Mr Ikari inclined his head toward me, but it was Lieutenant Pippin that he addressed. 'Mr Pippin, a report.'

Young Pippin snapped to attention. 'Yes, sir. Miss Berkeley, Mrs Fisher, Lieutenant Charpentier and I went for an early morning run, sir. Upon returning to the accommodation a table fell from the upper deck to strike Lieutenant Charpentier on the head. It narrowly avoided Miss Berkeley and was taken to be another deliberate attempt at causing her harm. I raced to the upper deck but was not able to locate the person that dropped the table. However, as Mrs Fisher and I came back to this level, we saw Mr Kenyon sneaking up behind Miss Berkeley.'

I had to hand it to Pippin, the report was given without bias or opinion. There was no conjecture to suggest he had seen something that he might not have seen or exaggeration to make his decisions sound more reasonable.

Ian Kenyon waited patiently for Mr Ikari's attention to swing in his direction, then started talking fast. 'I demand to be released immediately.

I have done nothing, know nothing about a table and when I get back to my suite I will be contacting my lawyer in the Hamptons and arranging for him to sue this cruise line and everyone that works for it so hard that I imagine I will own this boat by the time he has finished.' Mr Ikari opened his mouth to respond, but Ian Kenyon rudely steamrollered right over him. 'Furthermore, I have no interest in the life, or death, of the little blonde trollop that Tarquin Trebeck deemed worthwhile of bedding. I don't care that he is dead, but since you know that I didn't kill him, I don't see why you might think that I would want to kill her.'

All around him, the company of security guards bristled at the evil insults he had spewed toward Barbie. His threats to sue were nothing but hyperbole and I was sure they knew it. He was a guest though, so unless they could prove he was guilty of something, they couldn't touch him.

Mr Ikari was prepared to push his luck though. 'Mr Baker, Mr Schneider, please escort Mr Kenyon back to his accommodation...'

'I will go wherever I damn well please,' Ian started saying, but this time he was cut off by Mr Ikari.

'If he resists, gentlemen, please use the minimum force required to restrain him.' Then he looked directly into Ian's eyes. 'Mr Kenyon, I ask for your cooperation at this time. There has been a murder and at least one attempted murder. I don't know how you fit into these events, or even if you do. But I must interview you with regards to this morning's events, much as I did yesterday following Tarquin Trebeck's murder. I will detain you no longer than is absolutely necessary. Will you give me your cooperation, sir?'

With some reluctance, Ian Kenyon nodded his head. He was looking at the deck, wanting to rant more, but unable to in the face of Mr Ikari's reasonable and calm request.

'Perhaps, then, we should all get out of the rain,' suggested Mr Ikari.

Two of the guards that had arrived with Mr Ikari had been checking over Lieutenant Charpentier. Barbie had already been doing it, making sure he was breathing and comfortable but as two of the ship's EMT team arrived with full crash gear to deal with him properly, the guards kneeling next to her, helped her to her feet. Ian Kenyon shot her a look of disgust as he walked by her, but I don't think she registered it.

The only thing I wanted to do, was get Barbie back to my suite and look after her. Jermaine would go nuts when he found out she had been targeted again and I had to admit that I was irked by Ian Kenyon. Shane had fingered him as the killer and here he was in the right place at the right time to have dropped a table on Barbie's head, see it miss and then take a circuitous route around to come up behind her intending to finish the job.

I would let Mr Ikari question him again, but if Ian slipped off the hook once more, I might just have to do some sleuthing myself.

The first task for the guards was to take Pippin to the upper deck restaurant to identify the couple he had spoken with. Their testimony would condemn Ian Kenyon quite quickly if they had seen him throw the table over the side.

I wasn't invited but I didn't let that stop me and I kept Barbie by my side, her hand in mine as we followed Pippin and two other guards inside the familiar restaurant. The smell of breakfast assailed my nostrils, reminding me that I was already hungry before we set off for our run. The guards paused, waiting for Pippin to scan the room and I thought for a moment that he couldn't see the old couple he was looking for and that they might have already finished breakfast and left. Thankfully, they were simply tucked in a corner.

When I saw where we were heading, I realised that I knew the couple in question. They were Horace and Maureen something or other, an Irish couple I had spoken to over dinner a week ago and waved to several times since. Horace was a retired electrician, or was it a plumber? He had been something like that and Maureen was a primary school teacher.

As we made our way across the room, eyes tracked us, partly, I think, because there were two members of the ship's security detail and their white uniforms were worth looking at, but also because they were being followed by two bedraggled looking women and one man in sports gear.

'Good morning, sir, madam,' said the first guard to reach their table. 'Terribly sorry to bother you. I'm afraid I have to ask you a few questions about what you saw on the upper deck terrace this morning on your way to breakfast.'

'Hello, Patricia,' said Maureen, peering around the guards to wave at me. 'Terrible weather we're having, isn't it?'

The guard cocked an eyebrow at me. My presence wasn't helpful. Ignoring him, I said, 'Hi Maureen. Hi, Horace.' Horace winked and gave me a smile. 'The gentleman's question is quite important actually,' I pointed out, then stepped back so I was out of their eyeline and less of a distraction.

'As I was saying,' the guard resumed speaking. 'This is to do with what you saw this morning. Can you describe the man you saw, please?'

'Saw?' echoed Horace, his eyebrows raised in question. 'We didn't see anything. I like a puff on my pipe in the mornings, gets my lungs going, you see? So, we went outside and then the young fellow here appeared and asked if we had seen anything...'

'And you said you did,' insisted Pippin.

Horace bristled slightly. 'No, dear boy. I said we heard someone. Entirely different thing.'

Pippin opened his mouth to argue but shut it again. To start with, arguing with guests wasn't the done thing, especially not in such a public setting but it looked as if he was now questioning his own memory of the event. He had been charged with adrenalin and moving fast, maybe he had simply misheard them.

The guard that had spoken to Horace said, 'Terribly sorry to have bothered you, sir. Please enjoy the rest of your day.' He turned to go, shooting Pippin a sympathetic look that told him he was in trouble. He had attacked Ian Kenyon and didn't seem to have justifiable cause. Yes, he thought he was about to attack a member of the crew that we knew to have been threatened, but his reasons for believing Ian might attack Barbie were now thrown into doubt.

The guards went around me as I hadn't moved. Something was making the back of my skull itch. 'Horace, what did you hear?' I asked.

'Hmmm?'

'You said you didn't see anyone, but you heard them. What did you hear?'

'Oh, um.' Horace leaned back in his chair, one eyebrow raised while the other squinted and he thought about his answer. 'It sounded like a walking stick,' he said after a few seconds.

'Yes, that's right, love,' agreed Maureen. 'It sounded like a walking stick. It went click, click, click on the deck. The pace was slow, like an old person's shuffle.' I had to wonder what they considered to be old as they were both in their eighties.

I thanked them, and still holding Barbie's hand, left them to finish their cups of tea. The guards were waiting for us at the entrance to the restaurant. 'If you are ready to return to your suite, Mrs Fisher, we will escort you and Miss Berkeley there.'

'Thank you, yes. I believe it is time to get dry and my butler will have breakfast waiting for us.' The guards fell into step either side of us, one in front and one behind as we walked the short distance to my suite. I hadn't taken my door card with me so knocked for Jermaine to let us in.

'Madam?' he said in question as he took in our additional guards and the absence of Lieutenant Charpentier. Several minutes later, when I finished telling him about the table and Pippin's attack on Ian Kenyon, he asked, 'Were Lieutenant Charpentier's injuries life threatening, madam?'

I shrugged, but said, 'I don't think so.'

Satisfied, he said, 'Very good, madam. Shall I serve breakfast?'

I smiled at his ability to maintain normal routine no matter what went on around him. 'In just a few minutes, please, Jermaine. I would like to get dry. I'm sure Barbie and Pippin feel likewise.'

'We are leaving, Mrs Fisher,' announced the chattier of the two guards. Come to think of it, I wasn't sure I had heard or seen his partner speak at all. 'Lieutenant Pippin will be staying with you for now. Is there anything else you need?'

'For now? Will Pippin be replaced?' I asked, my voice hushed so Pippin wouldn't hear from his bedroom.

Now it was the guard's turn to shrug. 'That will be down to Mr Ikari. Incidents where a crew member assault a guest always result in dismissal. Even when there is just cause or reasonable doubt.' He turned to his colleague. 'Do you remember anyone ever getting away with hitting a guest?' he asked.

His silent colleague just shook his head.

The news horrified me. Pippin had acted in good faith and upon my instruction. I distinctly remember yelling for him to attack, urging him on when I saw Ian standing behind Barbie. I was going to have to speak up on his behalf, intercede with the captain and go over Mr Ikari's head if necessary. Surely the circumstances here were different. I realised the two men were waiting for me to dismiss them. 'Thank you, gentlemen. Have a good day.' Jermaine stepped around me to let them out and I took myself to my bedroom; I had so much to consider.

I got a shower and as I was towelling my hair dry, I heard raised voices coming from the other side of my bedroom door. As I came out of my bedroom, a towel still in my hands, it was Jermaine that spoke first.

'My apologies, madam. Mr Sussmann appeared at the door and he was too excited to be left in the passageway.' Shane was staring intently at me, desperate to speak.

I nodded for him to say his piece. 'Go ahead, Shane.'

'He tried it again, didn't he?' Shane blurted. 'Ian Kenyon, he had another go at killing Barbie, didn't he?' Shane was positively vibrating with excitement. When neither Jermaine nor I replied, he said, 'I've been doing research.'

Jermaine lifted a hand to touch his lips, a gesture intended to silently attract my attention. 'Breakfast is served, madam,' he said, when my eyes swung from Shane's face to his.

Looking back at Shane, I asked, 'Won't you please join us?'

'For breakfast? Sure. Always ready to eat. I'll tell you all about what I found out while we eat.' He glanced around to look for the table, and as he did so, he plucked a fork from an inside pocket of his jacket; he really was always ready to eat.

'There'll be no need for that, sir,' said Jermaine as he plucked the fork out of Shane's hand. 'You will find silverware waiting for you. How would you like your eggs, sir?'

As they discussed breakfast options, Jermaine escorted Shane to the indoor dining table. It was designed to seat twelve but had only ever had four around it during my stay. I went to check on Barbie. Jermaine had placed her in the bedroom nearest to mine. As I understood it, the ship had a wide selection of high-quality furniture in storerooms way down in the bowels of the ship so that it could accommodate the needs of any of its top clients. Some might have small children in need of cribs, or toddlers that would need appropriately sized beds with guards or whatever. Whatever the case, I guess that's why there was a bedroom so close to mine.

'How are you doing in there, sweetie?' I called out as I knocked on the doorframe and turned the handle.

Barbie was doing better than I had worried she might be. She was dressed in fresh clothes and had fixed her hair already, reminding me that mine would turn to frizz shortly and need straightening or pinning. 'I'm hungry,' she replied. 'Jermaine made it smell like breakfast. Did I hear Shane outside? Is he here because someone tried to drop a table on me?'

Her brain was bouncing around between different ideas, but she seemed fine for now. 'Let's get breakfast,' I suggested, hoping that something as normal as sitting down to eat would help her to settle.

She followed me back into the living area and toward the dining table where Shane was already sitting with an expectant look on his face. 'Hi, Barbie,' he said with a wave.

I motioned to Jermaine as Barbie took a seat and stepped to one side with him. 'I want you to join us for breakfast,' I whispered quietly. Now that might not seem like a big thing, but Jermaine was all about the ceremony of his job and the butler never ate with the lady, except maybe at Christmas, so I was asking him to be something that he wasn't. As his eyes widened in horror, I hissed, 'Barbie needs her friends close.'

I knew he wouldn't be able to present an argument, so I wasn't surprised when he nodded his acceptance and said. 'Very good, madam.'

'Is Pippin joining us?' I asked, looking around. The door to his bedroom opened when I looked at it. He was back in full dress whites, looking elegant and official even though the uniform needed taking in a bit.

He smiled at me, a melancholy expression hinting at the knowledge he carried – his job here was in severe danger. 'I thought I should get some wear out of it while I can,' he said with a forced half smile.

I patted his arm and looped mine through his to escort him to the table. 'Let's not assume the worst, eh? There are circumstances to consider.'

He forced the smile again, then said quietly so only I would hear, 'She's worth it.' Before I could say anything in return, he let go of my arm to grab my chair, pulling it back like a gentleman to settle me at the table. I took my seat and Jermaine began to serve breakfast.

The table was silent, so I initiated a conversation. 'Shane you said you had been doing some research. What is it that you think you found?' I asked.

He was already forking bacon onto his plate from the platter to his front but managed to look up. 'I know why Ian killed Tarquin,' he announced, putting the bacon tongs down to grab a spoon of scrambled egg. I thought I might have to prompt him to reveal more but once his plate was stacked high, and his face bore a satisfied look, he began talking. 'I had to delve right into his past. Tarquin's that is, not Ian's. I started researching Ian; the internet is a wonderful thing, isn't it? Surprisingly, there wasn't much to find about Ian. Lots a basic information but nothing that proved helpful so I started looking at Tarquin instead. Tarquin was signed up as a child actor and his original agent was Ian Kenyon. I guess Ian was in a different part of the industry at the time, but he was a much younger man then.'

'How long ago was this?' I asked.

'*Summer Adventure* was his first film and he was with Ian then, so I guess it was eighteen years ago,' Shane replied, his mouth half full of breakfast as he did.

Jermaine narrowed his eyes at the man's manners, but it went unnoticed. Shane was a little uncouth, but I felt an affinity for him; he clearly didn't have many friends, he wasn't very good looking and he would be off the ship and gone forever once we reached Hawaii in a couple of days. I could put up with him for that long if it made him feel wanted for a few days.

Next to me, Barbie took a sip of water to clear her mouth. 'If Ian was Tarquin's agent, surely he made good money. It was right after *Summer Adventure* that he started getting all the good roles,' she pointed out.

This time Shane swallowed before speaking. 'That's exactly right,' he agreed, nodding his head. 'Except that it isn't.'

'How so?' I asked, now confused. Had Ian made money or not and what exactly was the supposed motive for wanting to kill him.

Shane was only too happy to supply the answers. 'This is where is gets all legal,' he explained. 'Tarquin did start landing big movies. I think I read that he got paid fifty thousand dollars for his role in *Summer Adventure*, but got three hundred thousand for the next film, *On Falcon Rock*, and then three million for the film after that, *Home Invasion*, the one that really exploded his career.'

Barbie's brow was just as furrowed as mine. 'I still don't get it, Shane. As Tarquin's agent, Ian must have been making a fortune.'

'You would think so, wouldn't you?' he replied triumphantly. 'He didn't get a penny though. Because Tarquin was a minor, his mum, a single parent, signed the contract, but when the big bucks started rolling in, she hired a lawyer and got it revoked. Tarquin kept all the money.' He stuffed a forkful of bacon into his mouth and fell quiet as he chewed.

I flared my eyes at him. 'How, Shane? How did she get the contract revoked?'

I had to wait for him to swallow, then finally he explained. 'The contract was signed in California and she was under twenty-one at the time. Legally, she couldn't enter into the contract and it was Ian's responsibility to check such things, not hers. She was thirteen when she had Tarquin and her family disowned her. I guess they regret that now, but Ian Kenyon made Tarquin Trebeck famous, worked his butt off to land him roles that would propel him to stardom and he did so at the detriment of all the other actors he managed, dropping most of them to focus on his cash cow and then he got nothing for it. I think they even stiffed him with the legal bill.'

The table was silent. It was a spectacular revelation. Tarquin had got famous and Ian Kenyon had got nothing. Was it motive for murder? I guess that had to depend on the person, but it was certainly fuel for hatred and revenge.

'Is there any more?' asked Shane, mopping up the juice from his mushrooms with a finger. He had probably put away close to fifty percent of the food that Jermaine had served to the table. I was actually impressed.

Instead of answering him, I looked at Jermaine. Inside, I was muttering to myself. I was having an argument about whether I should do the thing that I thought I should do or do what I told people I would do.

'Is everything alright, madam?' asked Jermaine.

'Yeah, Patty,' chipped in Barbie. 'I can see your lips moving, but there's no words coming out.'

The internal argument ended at that point. 'I need to snoop. It might sound like a bad idea.' I chuckled at that point. 'It probably is a bad idea, but I am going to go with Shane's cleaning maid plan.'

'Really?' asked Shane, his head suddenly popping up from picking crumbs out of the bacon dish.

I nodded slowly, mostly to myself. I was going to do it. 'Jermaine, dear,' I said while running through the concept in my head. 'I need an outfit.'

'I'll go with you,' said Barbie. 'I want to know why he is trying to kill me.'

I place my hand on top of hers where it was resting on the table. 'You can't, sweetie. He knows you. I plan to go in when he is not there but if he comes back our cover will instantly be blown if he recognises you.' Shane opened his mouth and I knew he was about to volunteer too. 'It's the same answer for you, Shane.'

'But I'm invisible,' he countered. 'No one ever remembers or even notices me.'

'I'm sure that's not true,' I argued, not certain that it was. 'But there's too much risk. You are part of the film crew; he could easily recognise you. I will be going alone.' While it terrified me, it also felt like the safest option and the one least likely to end in disaster.

Ian Kenyon might be a murderer, bent on a trail of revenge, but even though there was a slim chance he had spotted me yesterday when I was spying on him, I was confident I could disguise myself and act in a manner that would alleviate suspicion.

Decision made, I slapped my hands on the table and stood up. 'The time to act is upon us,' I announced. I was feeling nervous and conscious that I was overcompensating because of it. Jermaine and Barbie, who knew me well enough to call me on it, were good enough not to.

'I'll make a call, madam,' said Jermaine as he too stood up. He didn't reach for his phone though. He started clearing plates instead. I wanted to push him to deal with the more pressing task first, but I refrained, telling myself that time was not a factor. If Barbie, was indeed his next target, then she was safe in my suite and we could pace ourselves.

The niggling doubt tickling the back of my brain was Mr Ikari's certainty of Ian Kenyon's innocence. What had he seen or been told that had given him such assurance? Whatever it was, I was going to challenge it. Barbie was part of my tribe and I would protect her with my life against anyone that threatened her. In a different world, she could be my daughter.

I looked about at Barbie, Shane and Pippin. 'If you will excuse me. I need to change.' I said as I moved away from the table.

As I walked away, Shane said, 'I guess there is nothing much I can do to help. If you need me, please just ask. I've written my number down in case I can be of assistance.'

I turned around to look at him because I could hear him walking toward the door. 'Don't worry, Shane. If he is guilty, we will get him.' I'm not sure what weight my confidence carried, but he gave me a thumbs up.

Jermaine followed the short, rather unique man to the door and closed it behind him. 'I have spoken with a friend on the cleaning crew, madam. Someone that cleans your suite actually. I expect to have a uniform delivered in the next fifteen minutes. Perhaps Miss Berkeley can help with your hair?' he suggested.

Curious, I said, 'My hair?'

Jermaine had to explain that, like many of the staff, the cleaning crew all wore their hair either very short or tied into a French plait. In order to look the part, my hair would also need to be plaited. However, it wasn't something I had done since my age ran to less than double digits. Thankfully, Barbie was up for the task.

'I haven't done this in a while,' she said as she settled in behind me at my dressing table. 'But I thought about a career in hair when I was younger, and I practiced different styles. This should be easy enough.'

As she brushed, separated and tugged my hair around, I thought about how the cleaners looked and acted. I realised though that I didn't really notice them. It bothered me that I had settled into a lifestyle where so much was done for me. It was nice, but it also made me a little uncomfortable. Jermaine said the person bringing a spare uniform was someone that cleaned my suite. I couldn't even picture the person's face. What did that say about me?

I had too many other things to worry about, so I pushed the concern from my mind and focused on what I was about to do. What else did I need to consider? To get into his cabin, I would need a master key. Had Jermaine already considered that? 'Jermaine?' I called loudly enough for him to hear.

The sound of his footsteps approaching ended when he came into my bedroom. 'Madam?'

'The cleaners must carry a master key of some kind, yes? I will need one of those, won't I?' I could remember seeing the cleaners, who were almost all ladies, letting themselves into rooms to perform their tasks. They would knock on the door, call out, then let themselves in using a door keycard attached on a cord to their belt. I guess they were attached for safety because no one wanted a master key getting into the wrong hands – like mine.

That was another reason I had to go alone; if Jermaine was caught with me, he would be in serious trouble with Mr Ikari. By myself, I could claim to have swiped the cleaner's outfit and the key.

'I have a key,' said Pippin. He was standing behind Jermaine, just inside my bedroom and peering around the side of the larger man. 'I can open the door.' He sounded glum, as if he had been contemplating what might happen when Ian Kenyon filed charges against him.

Helping me now wasn't going to do him any favours though. I said, 'I think you should distance yourself from what I am doing, Pippin. You need plausible deniability if I get caught. It's bad enough that you know about it, if I take your key, you will then be implicated in the crime.'

'I can obtain a key for you, madam,' said Jermaine just as we all heard a knock at the door. Jermaine departed to answer it, ushering Pippin from my bedroom as he did. My hair was done, Barbie satisfied with her work as she stepped back so I could turn my head to inspect it.

My blonde locks were pulled into a tight French plait that ended a couple of inches below my collar. Now I was going to have to get changed and hope the uniform fitted okay.

I followed Barbie into the living area of my suite to find the person that had brought the uniform and was surprised to find that it was a man. Jermaine already had the cleaning maid's outfit in his hand though his expression looked... what? Embarrassed. 'This is Ortise, Madam. Would you like to try the outfit on to ensure it fits? It is not quite what I expected, I'm afraid,' he said as he cut his eyes to Ortise.

I stepped forward to shake the man's hand. 'Nice to meet you, Ortise. Thank you for bringing this.'

Ortise had a very soft grip and an effeminate voice when he spoke. 'That's okay, sugar. I like dressing up too. Don't I, Jermaine?' he said with a sly smile and a wink at my butler.

Jermaine did not answer and still had an unhappy expression. Wondering what was bothering him, I soon found out when he handed me the outfit. A moment ago, when he used the word, I had thought it odd that he didn't say uniform. Now I knew why. What Ortise had brought for me was a saucy French Maid's bedroom outfit. Jermaine was staring into the distance, refusing to make eye contact and Ortise was giving me an encouraging smile. What did he think went on in my suite?

'Role play is such fun always,' said Ortise, nudging Jermaine's hip with his own.

Jermaine's expression didn't change but though it was hard to tell with his deeply tanned skin, I swear he blushed. I guess the term friend was a codeword for something else in this case. I allowed him his discretion though, but held up the garment as I said, 'I need a cleaners outfit to wear. I need to look like one of the cleaners.'

Ortise gave me a blank look for a second, then he got it and winked. 'Gotcha, sugar. To get into the role, it's got to be exact. I met couple like that before.' As my mouth dropped open, Jermaine took his friends arm and walked him across the room for a conversation. It looked short and rather one-sided. When it ended, Jermaine escorted Ortise back to where I was still standing. 'Jermaine says that I am confused and that I need to apologise for any suggestive comments I may have made.' The man's face was crimson.

Desperate to move on, I said, 'That's okay, Ortise. Thank you for bringing me this, but I really need to look like one of the cleaners.'

Ortise bit his top lip. 'That might take some time, sugar.' Jermaine nudged him again. 'Madam, I mean madam,' Ortise added quickly. 'There are very few ladies on the cleaning crew.'

My face scrunched in question to his answer. 'Really? I thought most of the cleaners were women?'

'No, sug... madam. Probably less than ten and they are all tiny girls from the Philippines. I'm not sure we will be able to get a uniform to fit you.'

Dammit, this was proving more difficult than I expected. 'Perhaps, madam, it would be prudent to abandon the plan?' suggested Jermaine, eager to keep me safe.

I held up the garment again. The black silk of the top ended with white lacey frills above the low-cut bra cups and came down to suspender straps to attach to stockings. They were detachable though, probably so one could wear hold-ups instead. The back of it was a giant lace like a corset.

'Goodness, that's racy,' said Barbie as she rejoined us.

She was right, but I pursed my lips and made a decision. 'Barbie, do you have any black leggings?'

Twenty minutes later I was wearing the offensive bodice but had accessorised it with black leggings and a thin black cardigan plus a pair of black running shoes. I turned in the mirror to inspect my backside, noting that somehow the black material made it look significantly bigger. My buttocks now looked like two balloons and because I had borrowed the leggings from Barbie, who was at least two dress sizes smaller than me, the material was stretched so thin the leggings almost looked like tights. The cardigan did a reasonable job of hiding the saucy maid outfit but there was no getting away from the fact that my boobs were hanging out of the top of it. Every time I leaned forward, they threatened to pop out. So much so, that it seemed my nipples were the only thing holding them inside, like they were gripping the material and holding on. The shoes were also Barbie's and a size too small. I could have just sent Jermaine to buy me some new ones but it seemed unnecessary and would delay my departure giving me more time to come to my senses.

Sighing because I knew it was the best I could do at short notice; I left my bedroom to see what the others thought. 'What do you think?' I asked the audience waiting in the living area.

Barbie smiled her huge beaming smile and clapped her hands. 'You look just like one of the cleaning crew, Patty.'

Pippin stared at my ample wobbly cleavage, caught himself doing so, felt his cheeks glow and cast his eyes down to stare at the carpet instead. They stayed there as he agreed with Barbie.

'Thank you, Ortise,' said Jermaine. 'I will arrange to return the garment later.' He made it clear that Ortise was expected to leave at this point, the obviously gay man grinning in a leering manner at the four of us, two girls, two guys, all dressed differently and, to his mind at least, about to have some kind of roleplay orgy despite what Jermaine must have said to him earlier.

'Have fun, everyone,' he sang as he let himself out.

Jermaine turned back to face me. 'Madam, the cleaning cart is waiting for you in the lobby and I have your keycard here,' he said as he held it up. 'I feel I must advise against this course of action though, madam. It seems... unnecessarily dangerous.'

'Yeah, Patty,' chipped in Barbie. 'I don't like it either. What if Ian did kill Tarquin and is trying to target me? Won't you be painting a target on your own back as well?'

'That will depend on what I find.' I had expected Barbie and Jermaine to do this; try to talk me out of it. 'Mr Ikari has dismissed him as a possibility. I have already challenged that decision and I don't see any point in doing so again now that Shane has brought new evidence to light.' The three faces staring at me were clearly sceptical. 'I will be careful,' I assured them. 'I look like a cleaner.' I corrected my statement upon seeing three sets of eyebrows simultaneously rise. 'Okay, I mostly look like a cleaner. I will be pushing a cleaning cart so I can use that to hide behind. No one will look at me anyway.' I added, thinking about how little attention I paid the cleaners. 'I am going to clean his room and while I do it, I will snoop around and see what I can find. I don't expect to find the murder weapon tucked in a drawer but maybe there will be something. If there isn't, I will finish cleaning and making up his bed and will leave.'

They still didn't look convinced. 'Look,' I said, starting to feel impatient with them, 'someone is targeting Barbie and I intend to find out who. By process of elimination if necessary. I'm starting with Ian Kenyon.' With that I walked through to the lobby where the cleaning cart was waiting for me. It was a large object loaded down with spare towels and bed sheets, all neatly folded into piles, and a large bin-like compartment in the middle for the dirty bedding et cetera to go in. Arranged around the outside were different cleaning fluids and cloths, a box of pillow mints and a black bin bag tied to the handle for litter.

'I will escort you, madam,' said Jermaine, moving to the door.

I held out a hand to stop him. 'It will look wrong if you are with me. I won't be long, don't worry about me. I am not the one being targeted.' Barbie would be safe enough in the cabin, Pippin was armed, and Jermaine was more than capable of defending her. Then I realised that Jermaine was overreacting because he wasn't able to do anything. Barbie had been targeted three times now, and he hadn't been around to help or even aware that she was in trouble. Now, I was going out and he wasn't allowed to do anything positive to help me either. He was agitated and it had taken me too long to recognise it.

I placed my hand on his arm. 'Look, Barbie is going to be with us for a while, certainly for dinner tonight. Perhaps you should ask her what she would like for dinner and make her something special.' That would give him something to focus on at least.

'Very good, madam,' he replied. 'Please be careful and be sure to call if you need me.' He handed me my phone, which I had completely forgotten, but then it was time to leave, butterflies arriving in my stomach as I pushed the cleaning cart into the passageway outside and started toward the elevators.

I got all the way to the elevator and into it before I remembered that I didn't know the name of Ian's suite. I had been there yesterday but hadn't thought to note what it was. All the doors had names or numbers on them, but there was an endless sea of doors to choose from. Muttering to myself, I went back to the suite, realised I hadn't picked up my handbag and therefore didn't have my door card. I used my head to knock on the door, rapping it twice with my forehead.

'What are you doing?' The question came from behind me, the voice that asked it was nasally and unpleasant to hear, and when I turned around to see who was there, I found a short, stern woman staring at me over the top of her glasses. Her hair was pulled into a tight bun and she wore a black suit, with black tights and flat shoes and her arms were folded in an impatient pose. 'Well?' she demanded. 'I'm waiting.' Then she took in my revealing top, her eyes bugging clean out of her head. 'What on earth are you wearing, girl?'

Then I saw the crew member badge on her lapel and read the title beneath it: Marianne Redmond Guest Services Manager. I was wearing a maid outfit and she was my boss. I was in so much trouble and I hadn't done anything yet. I dredged my brain for a lie that would work and, feeling defeated, I leaned back against the door for support and fell right through it. Jermaine had chosen that moment to open it.

'Goodness me,' said the stern woman. 'Which idiot employed you?' Then she looked at Jermaine. 'Is the resident in?' she asked.

Unusually stuck for words, Jermaine stuttered as he lied. 'Um, no?'

'Well, that's a relief. Come on, you,' she said, actually snapping her fingers at me. 'Chop, chop, girl. I haven't got all day. We can deal with what you have done to your uniform later.'

I struggled slowly to my feet, wanting to push by Jermaine on my way into the suite and have him shut the door on the awful lady, but it would take too much explaining so I kept my mouth shut and hoped that I could ditch her soon. Maybe she would take me in front of the elevators, and I would be able to jump in one and be gone before she could react. I exchanged a silent look with Jermaine and shook my head when he flared his eyes at me in question.

'Come on, girl. Hurry up and bring your cart.' She started walking away, in the opposite direction to the one I wanted to go. So much for diving in an elevator. 'What were you doing there anyway? I know the staff that work the upper deck and you are not one of them.'

'Um,'

'Come on, girl. Spit it out. I want an answer,' she snapped before I could even begin to offer her an answer.

I was getting angry and doing my best to keep a lid on it. 'Ortise is sick. He asked me to fill in.'

'Ortise? I spoke with him this morning. He wasn't sick then,' she argued but I could tell she wasn't expecting me to know the name of the person that should have been cleaning my suite.

'Yes, he said he had eaten something that didn't agree with him. I think it came on quickly. I'm not in any trouble for helping him out, am I?' I asked, filling my voice with false nerves and concern.

'We'll see.' Her reply was delivered to keep me feeling off guard. I could tell. She liked being the one with all the power. 'There's a mess to clean in the portside passage. I was on my way to assess what was needed but guess what? You volunteered.'

I trailed after her, struggling to control the heavy and unwieldy trolley because I had to rush just to keep up with her pace. 'Oh, dear, yes,' she said, finally slowing. I couldn't see what she was looking at, but I could smell it. Someone had imbibed one too many cocktails and then regurgitated them all on the carpet.

'Well? Don't just stand there, girl. Get it cleaned up.' She folded her arms again and stood to one side so she could watch. 'You can consider yourself under assessment.'

I looked at the mess on the floor and then back at the stern woman's face. I considered trying to clean it, I really did, but then the smell hit me again and as my stomach rolled, I decided what I was going to do. 'You clean it,' I offered her with a smile. I was already leaving, turning the trolley around so I could push it back the way I had come. It was shorter to keep going the way I had been headed but that meant going over the pool of vomit soaking into the carpet and I wasn't about to risk standing in it.

My response had caught the woman off guard, but she recovered quickly. 'Clean it myself?' she shrieked. 'Clean it myself? Get back here right now.'

'No thanks,' I called over my shoulder.

'I'll have your job!' she yelled after me.

I yelled back, 'I quit.' I couldn't help but smile as I said the words, turning a corner and leaving the stony-faced, old bat behind.

I arrived back at the elevator without further incident, travelled down just one deck and remembered once again that I didn't know which cabin Ian Kenyon was staying in. I had been so distracted by the stern woman I had forgotten again. I paused in the passageway, to dig out my phone; I wasn't going back upstairs to ask in person, that was for certain. But as the call connected and I absentmindedly chewed my lip, a door opened ahead of me and Ian Kenyon stepped out.

'Madam?' said Jermaine as he picked up the call. I didn't answer though; I was staring at the face of evil. The man I was sure had killed Tarquin was right in front of me, the same man that was now targeting Barbie for reasons I couldn't yet fathom. 'Madam?' asked Jermaine again, this time with urgency in his voice. I pressed the button to end the call as I watched the killer walk away down the passage, probably off to get some lunch or go for a drink, happy that he had gotten away with one murder and was plotting his next.

The second he was out of sight, I wheel the cleaning trolley to his door, swiped the doorcard and pushed his door open.

'I was starting to think you wouldn't show.'

I screamed and I swear a little bit of pee came out as my heart completely stopped, took a vacation and then returned just as suddenly, filling the void in my chest like a grenade going off under my ribs. It was only the cleaning trolley that kept me from collapsing.

I glanced to confirm the owner of the voice was who I thought it was, then gasped out, 'Shane, you scared the life out of me.' I was clutching my heart and using the trolley for support. When he left my suite earlier, the damned fool was only pretending to accept that he couldn't help me search Ian's room. He had clearly been waiting for me to arrive. However, when I turned to close the door, I caught sight of him, and it stopped me dead in my tracks.

I had to stand back to take it all in. I barely recognised him. His beard was gone, that was the first point to note and possibly the starkest because it changed the shape of his face. Where the hair had been, the skin now looked baby-bottom smooth, but he had nicked himself in multiple places, a couple of which still had tiny squares of tissue stuck to them. He had also shed his glasses, which distorted the face I knew even further.

The real shocker though was the cleaning maid's outfit he was wearing. Just like me, Shane had borrowed a French maid's naughty bedroom outfit. He must have got from a plus-size girl and even then, had needed to squeeze into it. The saucy outfit ended above his biceps, revealing hairy arms, and just below his junk, but he hadn't thought to wear leggings. His bare legs were milk bottle white and matted with thick ginger hair. I didn't want to look, but it was like seeing a car crash in slow motion; there was no option to look away.

'What are you wearing?' I asked, my heartrate returning to normal.

Shane grinned at me. 'I swiped it from one of the makeup girls. It's a bit tight. I think I popped a couple of stitches already, so I won't be putting it back.' He looked at my uniform and then at his and shrugged. 'It's not exactly right, but no one is here to see me anyway.'

He made a valid point, but I was still concerned that Ian might recognise him, and I was certain he would question whether the chubby man in the sex outfit was really in his suite to clean it. To get things moving, I said, 'We need to get on with this before he returns.' Then I pushed the cleaning trolley to one side so I could move into the room and I started looking around. There was a desk with a computer on it, much like the one in my room and it looked like the type of place a person might make notes.

'I'm going to, um… check the bathroom,' announced Shane as he stepped around me to go deeper into the suite.

I started leafing through the pieces of paper on Ian's desk, my boobs threatening to fall out each time I leaned forward so I had to hold one arm across my chest to keep them in place while I searched. The computer had been pushed to one side, the wireless keyboard and mouse stacked behind the monitor at the far left of the desk. Ian was one of those people who like to use pen and paper. I counted four A4 pads, each containing several pages of notes and I didn't need to read much to see that he was trying to write a script for a film. Did that mean anything? He was a producer, he used to be an agent, perhaps he had been a dozen other things in between but maybe what he truly wanted was to be a screen writer.

I scanned a few pages but none of the story ideas fleshed out in ink described a killer murdering a Hollywood star and then going after the girl he was interested in. Not that I expected a big smoking gun, but it would have been nice.

I rifled through the desk drawers, but I didn't find anything there either, so I went to check on what Shane was doing. I found him in the bathroom, just sitting on the edge of the bath. 'What are you doing?' I asked, mystified to find him doing nothing when he was so keen to get in here.

Startled by my voice, he looked up at me. 'I already looked in all the places in here,' he said, sounding defensive. 'I was taking a moment to think about where I might hide something I didn't want other people to find.'

'I thought about that too. I would ditch it over the side and be confident it was gone forever.'

'What if he wanted a trophy?' he asked. 'If I am right about his hatred for Tarquin and thirst for revenge being nearly two decades old, then he must also want to savour the victory. I know I would. I would want to keep something to remind me of the moment when I finally got my own back.'

'Ok,' I didn't believe it, but I was prepared to explore his theory with him rather than just poopoo it. 'Where do you think he would put something then?'

'Let's go look, shall we?' As he said it, he slapped the sides of the bath and got up, then slipped around me to head back into the suite. He was muttering as he started looking around, 'Maybe behind a ventilation panel or something.'

I couldn't fault his logic. The ventilation panel was screwed on tight though, no one was hiding a twisted trophy behind that without using tools and the screw heads looked unmolested. As Shane went into the bedside tables and pulled out the drawers, I said, 'I'll check under the bed.'

There was nothing there though. Not even dust bunnies and it was then that I spotted a fatal flaw in my plan. I was disguised as a cleaner and in his room under the ruse that I was there to clean it. However, it had already been cleaned today. The bed was made, the room was spotless, but as I began to panic, acknowledging that if Ian did return, he would know I was a fake. And just then I heard the all too familiar soft beep of the door lock opening.

I froze. Rooted in place by horror because I knew I was caught. Coming through the door, Ian shot me a smile. 'No need to stop, I forgot my smokes. I'll be just a moment.'

Too caught up in his own business, he hadn't questioned our presence. Maybe he would suddenly spot the incongruity later and question why there was a second cleaning crew in his suite. Right now, though, he was crossing the room to his desk to get his cigarettes.

Oh, lord, I thought, my heart banging in my chest; he was going to see that I had moved things. He didn't though. Without pausing, he grabbed the cigarettes, popped them into an inside jacket pocket and started back toward the door.

I was still frozen to the spot, unable to get over the shock of capture I felt when he walked in, but it wasn't my lack of motion that tipped him off, it was Shane. Shane yelled a cry of triumph and threw a drawer across the room.

'I knew it!' he exclaimed. 'I knew I was right.'

Ian's head shot around to look at Shane at the sound of his whoop so he witnessed the drawer being discarded and was looking at him when he spoke. 'What the devil is going on here?' he asked, glancing at me and then doing a double take. 'You!' he shouted, staring at me and looking angry. 'You're the one that was spying on me yesterday.'

'It's not what it looks like,' I replied weakly, the ridiculous phrase finding its way to my lips.

Then, across from me, I saw Shane fumbling in the hole the discarded drawer had left. I couldn't help but take my eyes from Ian to see what Shane was doing so I saw him reach under the chest of drawers and pull out a knife. 'What the devil is going on here? he asked. 'What the devil is

111

going on here?' he bellowed the question when he repeated it and held the knife aloft. 'We're catching a killer, that's what!'

'Got anything to say about my spying now, Mr Kenyon?' I asked. We had him. Shane had been right to suspect the film's producer and the research he had undertaken showed motive while the knife in his cabin might be the proverbial nail in his coffin.

Ian just stared at me, looking like a rabbit caught in headlights. But then he started laughing. 'I'm calling security,' he replied with a calm shrug.

'Good! They can lock you up!' yelled Shane. Ian had left the door ajar when he came in, intending to go straight back out but it had swung fully open behind him and Shane's loud voice was attracting attention from people in the passageway outside.

'Is everything alright?' asked a gentleman with a trimmed white beard and glasses, leaning through the open doorway to see what all the fuss was about.

'Come away, Bernhard,' called an unseen woman, presumably his wife but it was too late for that. Bernhard had seen Shane in his ridiculous outfit and the deadly-looking knife in his hand.

'Oh, my goodness!' he exclaimed, drawing the attention of his wife, who, now inquisitive, poked her head around the doorframe as well.

Then she screamed.

If Shane's excited yelling hadn't drawn enough attention, the woman's scream certainly did. Heavy boots were running along the passageway as she backed away pointing. 'He's got a knife,' she said, turning her head to blab the news to whoever was running towards her.

I made a guess which turned out to be right as two white uniformed members of the ship's security arrived at the door. This could not have gone worse. I opened my mouth to get my story in first, but then shut it again. Nothing I could say was going to make any difference.

'These two are imposters,' Ian claimed as he pointed to Shane and me. 'The woman,' a term I felt was derogatory, especially the way he said it, 'was spying on me yesterday. Now I find her in my cabin posing as a cleaner so she and her fat friend can plant a weapon.'

I recognised both members of the security team, a man and a woman, and hoped they knew who I was, but I didn't know their names. The woman was nearest to Ian and took the lead, holding up her hands in a calming gesture. 'Slow down, please, sir. You say this lady was spying on you? And now she is trying to plant a weapon?' she turned to his colleague. 'I think we need Mr Ikari,' she said, then added, 'Now.' When the man didn't react, prompting him to step out into the passageway to use his radio. I could hear him outside moving people on as a small crowd was beginning to gather. Then the female lieutenant brought her attention back to the room. 'Put the knife down please, sir.' The instruction was clearly aimed at Shane who was gleefully smiling as if certain he had found Tarquin's killer.

Thankfully, just as I saw the lieutenant's hand twitch towards his sidearm, Shane said, 'Sure. Where would you like it. This is valuable evidence.'

Ian scoffed, causing all three of us to look at him. 'Whose fingerprints are on it?' he asked, a wry smile playing across his lips. 'I know mine won't be because I have never seen it before. So, since you are holding it, I don't see how you hope to tie it to me.'

113

Shane fielded the question. 'We found it in your room. Hidden beneath a chest of drawers where no one would find it. Your little memento to celebrate how you killed the man that diddled you out of a fortune.'

Ian looked shocked. 'What on earth are you talking about man?' he demanded to know. The security officer was curious too.

This time I answered. Explaining what we knew about Tarquin making it big because Ian promoted him but then his mother finding a loophole to get out of paying Ian his cut. By the time I had finished the story, I could hear the guard outside addressing someone and then the unmistakeable sound of Mr Ikari's voice.

Even though I had caught the killer, I couldn't help but feel embarrassed at the steps I had taken to get here. I had promised that I would not involve myself, but Mr Ikari had assured me Ian Kenyon was not involved in Tarquin's death and here he was with what looked like the murder weapon hidden in his room.

As I steeled myself to defend my actions and stood up straight so I could look haughtily down, Mr Ikari came through the door and into the cabin, flanked on his left side by Lieutenant Baker. He took one look at me and bowed his head. He sighed and physically deflated as if he would have preferred it was anyone else in the room. Then, without another glance at me, he spoke to Lieutenant Baker, 'Take them both into custody please.'

'What!' I asked, my voice coming out as a surprised high-pitched squeak. Looking relaxed, Ian Kenyon was grinning like the Cheshire cat as he looked at me and I felt my confidence slipping as I asked, 'What do you mean, take us into custody? We found the murder weapon. It was hidden beneath his chest of drawers.'

As Baker began reluctantly to move toward me looking very apologetic, Mr Ikari held up his hand to make him pause. 'Mrs Fisher,' he said, pausing as I breathed in deeply and my boobs threatened to pop out again. He wasn't the only one that stared at them though, Baker and the female guard standing behind him looked as well, drawn to the impending disaster.

My face flushing, I said, 'Sorry,' and turned away so I could jiggle myself back into the stupidly low-cut cups.

When I turn back to face him, Mr Ikari picked up where he had left off. 'You have conducted an illegal search of Mr Kenyon's room. Even if that is the murder weapon, which I very much doubt it is, Mr Kenyon has an alibi for the time of Mr Trebeck's murder. He is not guilty, and you assured me you would not interfere in my investigation. No court in the world would allow the knife as evidence because of your illegal search and I am led to believe that Mr Sussmann has handled it, thus almost certainly destroying any fingerprints that may have been left by the murderer.'

I started to speak, but he held up a finger to silence me.

'Furthermore, since we are at sea and you have gained entry to this room, I can technically charge you with piracy. You have caused me quite the dilemma, Mrs Fisher and I am not pleased about it.'

I had nothing I could think of to say, but Shane said, 'Hold on. Let me check something. You are telling me that I am a pirate now?' His expression was just as gleeful now as it had been when he found the knife.

Mr Ikari gave him a look like he was dirt and strode from the room. 'You know where to take them,' he said over his shoulder without looking back.

My mouth hung open. I was in the wrong? How on earth was I in the wrong? A man had been murdered and I had found motive and a weapon.

Okay, I understood that we had maybe gone about finding the weapon in an unconventional way, but it had still been found. Whatever alibi Ian was using must be false, or they are wrong about the time of death. Or something.

'What is it that Bhavana holds over you, Ian?' I asked.

'Mrs Fisher, please,' begged Lieutenant Baker. He was waiting for me to move. It was time to leave Ian's cabin, but I wanted an answer.

'She knows you did it, doesn't she? Is she the one that provided your alibi?' Suddenly I saw the obvious truth of it. 'Oh, my goodness. That's it, isn't it. She knows you killed him but has given you an alibi. Why though? Are you influential enough to secure her next role?'

'Mrs Fisher, please,' Baker said again, this time with far more insistence.

'No, Baker, listen to me,' I insisted. 'I overheard Bhavana threatening to ruin... no destroy, that was the word she used, wasn't it?' I asked rhetorically while I stared at Ian Kenyon. 'Destroy. She has evidence that will destroy Ian if it gets out. She knows he did it.' Baker looked conflicted and the guard next to him was waiting for his lead. 'Call, Mr Ikari,' I begged. 'Ask him who Ian's alibi is.'

I could see he was wavering. He had his orders to carry out, but he knew me. He knew me well enough to believe that I might be right.

'Are you listening to this nonsense, man?' asked Ian, his tone dripping with derision. 'God, man. You have your orders. Get them out of my room.'

'One question,' I begged again. 'If I am wrong you can take me out of here in cuffs.'

'And make us walk the plank, aaaarrr,' laughed Shane behind me, clearly not understanding the gravity of our situation. I felt like hitting him with something.

Baker was staring at me, Ian was staring at him, but as Baker leaned his head down to speak into his lapel microphone, I let go a breath I hadn't realised I was holding. As he began to speak, he stepped around his colleague to have his conversation in the passageway and not be overheard.

'This is utter nonsense,' spat Ian angrily.

I couldn't really hear what Baker was saying, but when he came back in, he looked disappointed. 'If you please, Mrs Fisher,' he said as he held out his hand. Then he glanced at the female guard still waiting silently for instructions and said, 'Lieutenant Bhukari, you will accompany me.' She fell into position to his side, allowing enough space for Shane and I to exit the cabin but close enough to react if we tried to run or looked likely to do anything silly.

Sounding pleased with himself, Ian said, 'Thank you. Finally.' Then he patted his pockets and got ready to follow us out. 'I assume there will be a real cleaning crew along soon to completely scrub my room.' The comment was aimed at the guards, but he was looking at me when he said it.

Behind me, Shane finally got that this wasn't a joke. 'No,' he said. 'No. what are you doing? He's the killer!'

Baker was holding out an arm to guide me from the room. Silently, I complied. There really was nothing left to say. As I left Ian's cabin, he was telling the guards that he wanted to press charges. Shane refused to leave though, insisting that Ian was the killer and he wanted justice done for his childhood friend.

Baker and Bhukari were going to have to wrestle him from Ian's cabin if I didn't intervene. I walked back to the door. 'Come along, Shane,' I called. 'It's time to go.'

'But...'

'It's time to go,' I insisted quietly. My motherly tone did the trick, the young man accepting that there was no way to win this time. He gave in and allowed them to escort us away to wherever it was we were being taken.

Walking in the opposite direction, Ian started whistling to himself.

Baker and Bhukari walked us along the passageway and across and intersection before Baker asked us to stop. He produced a keycard and swiped us into a room that had no windows and no decoration. There was a table and chairs in the centre of the room and two bench seats against the wall to our left. The door we came in through was the only way out. It was an intimidating place to find oneself.

'What are we doing here?' I asked.

It was Baker that answered. 'Waiting for Mr Ikari I believe. He instructed me to bring you here but did not tell me why. Please make yourselves comfortable.'

Comfortable? I was feeling far from comfortable. Mostly I was conducting an argument in my head where one side of my brain wanted to berate me for ever leaving my suite. The suite was comfortable, the suite had Jermaine and Barbie in it. The suite had a TV. The other side of the argument was that someone kept trying to kill Barbie, a friend I was coming to love quite dearly. Evidence was pointing to Ian Kenyon, so of course I had left the safety of the suite to investigate. How could I not?

'Can I get you a drink of water, Mrs Fisher?' asked Baker. He was a love, but I shook my head no. I didn't want to have to ask to go the bathroom if we were going to be stuck in here for some time.

I pulled out a chair from the table and sat down to wait. Shane paced and the two lieutenants took up position by the door. Both of them looking like sentinels. Ten minutes that felt more like sixty slowly ticked by until finally a quiet knock was followed by the door handle turning. Mr Ikari came into the room, flanked by two more people in white uniform, one of which was a woman I had not seen before.

I wanted to stand up and start talking, but I remained in my chair and waited for Mr Ikari to speak. I was very much on the back foot and unwilling to rile him.

'Mrs Fisher, I believe you know Lieutenants Baker and Bhukari.' I had heard others address the female officer already, but her name hadn't registered. Now I would remember it. 'They will be leaving us now.' He turned and spoke quietly to the two guards, so quietly, in fact, that I could not hear the exchange in the small room. Then Baker and Bhukari both left, leaving me with Mr Ikari and the two unfamiliar persons in white uniform. I was beginning to feel nervous.

'Mr Sussmann, please take a seat.' The request was delivered in a firm tone and Shane complied, quietly pulling out a chair and sitting adjacent to me. The three people in uniform were still standing. Mr Ikari indicated the female officer to his right. 'This is Commander Shriver. Commander Shriver works in our legal department and had drawn up some paperwork for you to sign.' The woman was tall and thin, and her features were a little androgynous. I could tell the person inside the uniform was a woman but a flat chest and a face bereft of makeup made the distinction questionable. At first glance I thought many might get it wrong.

I hadn't seen the briefcase she was carrying until she raised it and placed it on the table. My eyebrows were fighting their way to the very top of my head. Why was I signing paperwork? What kind of paperwork was it?

The catches on the briefcase sprung open with a familiar double click noise and the woman opened it with it facing away from me so I couldn't see its contents. No one said anything as she removed two identical plastic folders, each filled with paper.

It was Mr Ikari that finally broke the silence. 'I have information that I am prepared to share with you, Mr Sussmann, Mrs Fisher, but I will not do so until you have signed this paperwork.'

'What is it?' Shane asked before I could.

Commander Shriver laid the two folders on the table, one in front of each of us. 'It's a gagging order, essentially,' she explained. 'If you later divulge what you hear today, you will be liable for prosecution.' My goodness, what on earth were they going to tell us? I was all but bursting to hear what they had to say, but I had no way of knowing what I was really signing. Surely, I needed a lawyer present just to explain my rights?

As I stared at the paperwork and Shane picked his up, I heard a knock at the door. The male security guard opened it to reveal the captain framed in the doorway. He looked directly at me and I felt my cheeks flush with heat. Quickly I glanced southwards to make sure I was showing as little cleavage as possible.

'Mrs Fisher,' he said in greeting as he doffed his hat and stepped inside.

'Alistair,' I replied by way of acknowledgement, but I didn't say anything else. I wasn't going to apologise for trying to defend Barbie, but I knew I had betrayed the captain's trust. The guard closed the door again, but unlike the other crew members, who remained standing, the captain took a seat next to me. He took in my outfit, his eyes glancing at but not dwelling on my chest. 'Well, I guess I now know who it was that Mrs Redmond wanted to sack. That's one mystery cleaned up at least.' As I turned scarlet, he forced a half smile as if he was having a tough day and putting a brave face on it. Then he did something that surprised me; he took my hand.

My hands had been resting on the table, gripped together to keep them from fidgeting nervously, but he reached across and slipped his warm, supple hand into mine and held it. Somewhere between shocked and exhilarated, all I could do was stare at him.

'Is the paperwork signed?' he asked but the question wasn't aimed at me and it was Mr Ikari that answered, 'Not yet.'

With his free hand, Captain Huntly reached across to open the plastic folder nearest to me then asked for a pen. 'There is nothing untoward going on, Mrs Fisher. I have been concerned for your well-being and consider myself to blame for your... activities today. Had I confided in you earlier, it would have been possible to avoid all this.' He indicated the room and our current situation. 'I am however, under a gagging order myself, as is everyone in this room, so I am faced with a dilemma. I can either bring you inside the circle or can lock you in your suite until we reach Hawaii. I would much rather it was the former than the latter.'

He pushed the paperwork toward me and offered the pen. 'That goes for you too, Mr Sussmann. It occurs to me that it might be simpler to lock you in our brig for your actions, but I would much rather not do so.'

'What is going on?' Shane asked in a hushed breath.

Slowly, the captain extricated his hand from mine, the warmth of it staying with me for a moment as I lied to myself that I was glad he had finally let go. 'That I cannot tell you. Either of you, until you sign the paperwork.'

I couldn't say that I was convinced it was a good idea to sign the forms in front of me, but I was way too curious to resist doing so. As I picked up my pen, scanned the first page and started signing my name, Shane picked up his paperwork and did likewise, neither of us attempting to read the dozen or so pages of legal speak the pages contained.

122

As I put the pen down, Commander Shriver picked up the paperwork, quickly checked it and placed it back inside the plastic folder and then inside her briefcase. Then she did the same with Shane's and gave the captain a curt nod.

As the briefcase closed with a different but equally familiar double click, the captain started talking. 'The reason, Mr Ikari is so certain that Ian Kenyon is innocent, is that he was being filmed at the time of Mr Trebeck's murder.'

'Filmed?' My brow crinkled as I asked the question, unsure that I had heard him correctly.

'Ian Kenyon is involved in a sting operation orchestrated by the FBI who are operating on board the Aurelia with my permission. At the time of Mr Trebeck's murder, Ian Kenyon was in bed with Bhavana Navuluri.' That made my jaw drop. Bhavana was stunning, one of the most beautiful women I had ever seen in person and she was sleeping with Ian Kenyon? A balding, fifty something year old man with a belly roll, glasses and a weak chin. The equation didn't balance. 'Bhavana has been operating a honey trap,' the captain explained. 'Using her looks, she lures influential men to her bed and then tricks them into performing a forced sex routine.'

Forced sex? 'You mean...' I didn't want to say the word.

'Bhavana had Ian mock rape her at her request and filmed it so that it looked as if she was the victim of a rape. She is using the film to blackmail Mr Kenyon.'

'For money?' I asked.

The captain shook his head. 'For film roles. The FBI believe she has already gathered evidence of the same form to blackmail a number of other A list directors, actors and agents across Hollywood. Gathering evidence though has apparently been impossible because the men involved are married and, in most cases, have children. She preys on their fear, not only of prosecution, but of losing their family so when the FBI approached men they believed to be her victims, they all refused to talk.'

'This explains her meteoric rise over the last two years.' It was the first time Shane had spoken in a while and I had all but forgotten he was there. 'No wonder she gets roles even though she can't act.'

'Why hasn't she been arrested already?' I asked.

The captain nodded his head at my question, perhaps acknowledging that it deserved an answer. 'They are waiting for Bhavana to accept payment in the form of favourable treatment and to capture evidence of her blackmailing him.'

'I heard her,' I blurted, startled to connect the dots between what I heard them arguing about at the prow of the ship yesterday. 'They were arguing about it yesterday. I stumbled upon them when I went for a walk yesterday. She threatened to destroy him with the evidence she had from his activities the night before. I thought she had seen him kill Tarquin.'

This time the captain pursed his lips. 'Mr Kenyon told me about that. I guess you were the one spying on him.' My cheeks flushed. 'He was fitted with a hidden microphone but there was too much background noise from the wind at the front of the ship. He thought he had her, but the recording is useless. It is only a matter of time before she repeats her demand though. The FBI just need to be ready, and of course they want to make sure their case is iron clad.'

Iron clad. That was what Mr Ikari had called Ian's alibi. I hadn't believed him. At least no one had been hurt. But then I remembered

Tarquin and Barbie. 'So, who killed Tarquin and why are they now targeting Barbie?'

Captain Huntley glanced at his number two, the look they exchanged meaning something I did not understand. Then he stood up, regaining his feet and collecting his hat from the table. It was Mr Ikari that spoke though. 'We do not have an answer to that yet, Mrs Fisher. I can assure you that we are working on it. The guards in your suite will be rotated later today to keep them fresh. I am confident that two armed guards will keep Miss Berkeley safe.'

I nodded along, wondering who could be the killer now that I knew it was not Ian Kenyon.

Next to me, Shane said, 'So, Ian didn't kill Tarquin?'

Mr Ikari tilted his head slightly, wondering what more evidence he needed to produce. 'Um, no, Mr Sussmann. No, he did not.'

'Then how did the knife get into his room?' Shane countered.

Mr Ikari fixed him with a steely gaze. 'Yes, I've been wanting to ask you about that. Did you take the knife into the room with you and plant it as evidence?'

Shane's eyes bugged out of his head. 'What?' he screeched. Mr Ikari just stared at him. 'I would never do such a thing,' Shane stated with as much conviction as he could manage. I could tell that Mr Ikari didn't believe him, but then I didn't either. Shane had been after Ian Kenyon right from the start. I didn't know why, but I could believe that he had snuck the knife in with him and slipped it under the chest of drawers so he could produce it and claim it had been there all along.

Captain Huntly leaned in close to Mr Ikari and whispered in his ear. Then turned to face Shane and me. 'I must go. I have other matters to attend to. Please do try to keep yourself out of trouble, Mrs Fisher. I much prefer to meet with you socially.' He indicated about the room to show how it conflicted with his ideal, but yet again I couldn't help but feel that his comment about meeting with me socially was unnecessary. It felt like he was flirting with me, but he was no longer looking my way, instead focused on the man next to me. He nodded his head and said, 'Good day, Mr Sussmann.' Then winked at me. 'Mrs Fisher.' His hat went on his head and he went out the door, the guard holding it open for him and closing it again afterward. I continued to stare at the closed door, confused not only by the handsome captain's actions, but also by my own reaction to it.

Mr Ikari broke my train of thought. 'I think that will do for today. Mr Kenyon is, of course, not pressing charges for your invasion today. I must ask though, with the most strenuous insistence, that you do not try anything like this again. Either of you,' he added. 'But most especially you, Mrs Fisher. This is hardly your first offence.' When neither of us said anything, he clapped his hands together and said, 'Do you wish to be escorted back to your suite, Mrs Fisher?'

'What about me? Don't I get escorted?' asked Shane.

His question earned him a single raised eyebrow from Mr Ikari and the reply, 'Not unless you are going to Mrs Fisher's suite, no.'

Once again, I found myself feeling sorry for Shane. He meant well, he just said the wrong thing a lot and rubbed people up the wrong way. I doubted Jermaine would be enthralled, but I was going to invite the poor soul back to the suite for some dinner. 'Would you like to join me for some afternoon tea?' I asked him, hitting with an endearing smile. What can I say? He brought out the motherly side of me. 'Perhaps we deserve a drink as well,' I suggested. 'Do you like gin?'

A minute later, I had bid Mr Ikari and his subordinates goodbye and was being escorted back to my suite by Shane instead. We drew a lot of looks, dressed as we were and my hand looped into his elbow. But no one stopped me to request I deal with a mess anywhere, so we made it back to the sanctuary of my rooms without further incident. Approaching my door, I felt my heart sink as I remembered that I hadn't brought my keycard with me, then chuckled at myself as I remembered I had a universal one. It was tucked into a pocket and it opened my door just as it had Ian's.

'Jermaine, I have a guest for tea,' I called out as I closed the door behind me. I shucked my shoes, glad to take them off as they had been pinching my feet for what felt like hours now, but as I scrunched my toes into fists and wriggled them to free them off, I noticed the bloody handprint on the doorframe leading from the lobby into the suite's living area and my heart stopped beating.

I called out, 'Jermaine,' again as I nervously peered into the living area. 'Jermaine, are you okay?'

'Something amiss?' asked Shane. He was behind me in the lobby still, taking off his shoes because I had taken off mine. I pointed to the blood. I heard him suck in his breath and make a retching sound. He swore and put his hand on the wall to steady himself. 'Whose blood is that?' he asked.

I didn't know, but I hadn't had an answer from Jermaine after calling for him twice and I was getting a very bad feeling. I reached behind me to grab Shane's arm and pulled him with me as I crept into the suite.

There was a blood trail going across the carpet in the living area. It started just in from the lobby and got progressively more convincing as it went. At first a few drops, but then a thin trail and then more than a thin trail. Whoever had left it was bleeding badly. I could hear Shane making quiet gagging noises behind me and I worried he might faint. I needed him. I had no idea what we were about to find, but I didn't want to deal with it by myself.

I was just about to call out again and send Shane to get help when I heard a shout. I say shout but it was more like an enraged snarl. 'Leave him!' The woman's voice came from one of the bedrooms, but I had been facing the wrong way and couldn't be sure which one it was. Until I saw the bloody handprint.

It was on Barbie's door!

'Get help,' I hissed at Shane as I let go of his arm.

'No. I'm staying with you,' he hissed back.

128

I shook my head. 'You're as white as a sheet. Go get help before you pass out,' I insisted. He meekly nodded his acceptance and started back toward the door, taking care not to step in the blood seeping into my carpet.

'Just tell me why!' the woman screamed again. 'Why did you take him from me?'

Then I heard Barbie's voice, instant relief washing through me when I heard her say, 'I don't know what you are talking about.'

'Yes, you do!' the woman bellowed.

Readying myself against what I might find beyond Barbie's bedroom door, I pushed it open, calling out, 'Is everything alright in here?' I made my voice sound light and unconcerned as if I hadn't seen the blood.

'Patty get out! She's got a gun!' yelled Barbie, unseen inside the room until I took another step inside. The scene in the bedroom was like something from a movie. Pippin was on the far side of the room being cradled by Barbie. Laying on the carpet, his white uniform drenched with blood below his stomach, he looked deathly pale. He was conscious and being propped up by Barbie who was wearing nothing but a pair of panties; she must have been getting changed when the attack happened. Pippin's face was scrunched against the pain he must be feeling, and I could see his holster hanging open so the gun twitching between them and me was his.

There had been no smell of cordite when I came into the suite though, so he hadn't been shot. As that thought flickered through my brain, I spotted a discarded knife on the carpet by the feet of the woman holding the gun. She was twenty feet away, over by the far wall of the room where she could pin Barbie and Pippin in place. The woman's face was an

129

ugly, tear-streaked mess but she was holding the gun in hands that were steady.

'Who are you?' she demanded.

I held my arms out to my sides, showing her my empty hands. 'Let's all just take it easy, please,' I begged, trying to make my voice as soothing and calm as possible even though my heart was pounding in my chest. 'I'm Patricia. I'm Barbie's friend. Why don't you tell me who you are?'

It was the wrong question though. I saw her snap as she started laughing. 'You see! You see! That's exactly the problem. You don't know who I am because she took him from me.' She emphasised who she meant by jabbing the gun toward Barbie and keeping it trained on her, lining the barrel up and squinting down her arms at her target.

Then I worked out who the woman was. She was slender and pretty and somewhere in her early twenties. Her skin was flawless and her hair perfect. She had on a floaty, but elegant summer dress and bore the look of someone whose life revolved around looking good. When I added those observations to the cast on her lower left leg, I knew she was the original actress playing the part that Barbie ended up with. I hadn't paid any attention to the film crew or the actors until Barbie had been picked from the crowd by Tarquin and asked if she could act. It happened after the original actress slipped by the pool and broke her ankle. Then I remembered what Horace and Maureen said. They heard a click, click noise like an old person's walking stick. Except it wasn't a walking stick they had heard; it was this woman's crutch.

'Barbie didn't do this to you,' I said gently.

'This was going to be my big break,' she sobbed. 'The world would see me with Tarquin Trebeck and the roles would flood in. And we would have been seen together on the red carpet. We would have been a perfect

Hollywood couple, starring in movies and... and everything.' She sniffed deeply, forcing tears back as she realigned the gun that had been starting to drop.

'You were sleeping with him,' I confirmed, more to myself than to anyone else.

Her head swung to stare at me, but her gun arm didn't move. 'And he dumped me the second the blonde slut showed up. Suddenly I was yesterday's news. She ruined everything. So, I'm going to kill her.'

The way she said the words made me believe her. She was capable and determined. I couldn't tell what was holding her back, but she was going to do it soon if I didn't work out how to stop her. I took a pace closer, but the gun instantly swung to me. 'Don't move. I can kill you too if you like.

On the floor, Barbie was soothing Pippin and stroking his hair. He was going to bleed out we didn't get him help soon. Barbie looked up at the crazy woman. 'He's not part of this. Let me get him help. Please,' she begged.

Then Shane spoke. He was standing behind me, the sound of his voice making me jump. 'Cindy, put down the gun.'

The woman curled a lip and cocked an eyebrow at him. 'How do you know my name?' she wanted to know.

'I worked with you on the film set, Cindy. I'm Shane. We spoke just a few days ago. I know what it feels like to not get what you think you deserve. The movie industry is a meat grinder, chewing up dreams and spitting out nightmares.'

'What do you know about it?' she spat. 'You're a no one. I could have been a someone.'

'No,' Shane replied, his voice friendly. 'I was famous once. I was someone with a bright future and everyone knew my name. Now no one knows who I am, and no one remembers me. What you are going through now is no different to the sufferings of every other actor left out in the cold. Killing the girl that replaced you won't fix your career.' The gun arm, which had been pointing at Barbie was beginning to droop just a little. She was talking to Shane and he was beginning to get through to her. 'Let me help you,' he said as he took a step toward her.

'No.' Her answer was delivered with a note of finality. 'No, I want to know why she did it. I will get my answer and if you try to stop me, I will kill you.' The gun was pointing back at Barbie's head.

'I already told you. I didn't steal him from you. I didn't even know about you and all we ever did was kiss a couple of times.' Barbie's reply was a murmur. She was hugging poor Pippin, but he looked to have lost consciousness now, his eyes closed and his body slumped.

'Liar!' she screamed, spittle flying from her lips. 'You lured him in with your insanely perfect boobs. He couldn't be with me because he couldn't get out from under them.' Cindy did have a flat chest, I noted, but that was hardly Barbie's fault.

'I need to get him to a doctor,' Barbie implored the crazy woman.

'He looks dead,' said Cindy. 'Just like Tarquin. He deserved to die for what he did to me. Now, put the boy down and stand up,' she commanded. Then, when Barbie failed to move, she twitched the gun and fired a round into the wall behind her. We all jumped but Barbie screamed in shock. 'I said get up,' Cindy repeated her previous order.

Shane and I were rooted to the spot. Cindy was too far away for us to get to her without her first shooting one or maybe all of us. Seeing no option, Barbie gently slid Pippin from her lap and onto the carpet so she could stand up. Her bare skin was covered in Pippin's blood.

'One last chance, slut. Tell me why you stole Tarquin, or I'll kill your friends first and then kill you.' Three seconds ticked by and she spoke again. 'Last chance.' Then swung the gun away from her to point it at Shane and me. But Shane was already moving when she pulled the trigger, bursting into action as he sprinted across the room at the crazy woman. The thundering sound made me jump again and it might have stopped Shane in his tracks if he hadn't already built up enough momentum to carry him the remaining distance.

I saw Cindy's eyes widen half a second before he crashed into her, forcing her weapon arm up and slamming her into the wall. He had her! He was short and he looked out of shape, but he was heavier and stronger than the petite actress. She didn't stand a chance.

Except that he hadn't accounted for the crutch she had had hooked over her arm. As she realised she was going to lose the gun, she grabbed the crutch and smacked him in the nuts with it. He had his back to me, so I saw the end of it emerge from between his legs and heard his sharp outrush of air.

His grip on her faltered and too late I saw that I should have followed him across the room. My feet hadn't moved in the handful of seconds since she fired her second shot and now it was too late. As she hit Shane again and he started to sag, her other arm brought the gun back down to point at me. I sucked in a gasp of panic, certain she was going to shoot and that was when Barbie hit her with the Ottoman.

The large wooden storage chest with its embroidered top had been minding its own business at the end of the bed until Barbie took advantage of Cindy's momentary distraction. It had to weigh sixty pounds and it was three feet across. Barbie, graceful yet strong from many, many hours in the gym, had lifted it with one hand and swung it like a bat.

The gun went off as Cindy bounced away, the bullet making a neat hole in the ceiling and this time I did move, running toward the danger though my brain insisted I should go the other way. Cindy was scrambling for the gun which had gone skittering from her hand. She didn't get it though because Barbie stepped over her and kicked it away. Cindy was howling and swearing but she was disarmed. She didn't even have the crutch any more as Shane ripped it from her grasp and threw it away.

The sound of feet and Jermaine's panicked voice rang through from the living area and half a second later his worried face burst into the bedroom. He looked about with a dread expression until he saw that none of us were hurt. Barbie flashed him a weak smile and I said, 'It's okay,' putting a hand on his arm to reassure him. 'Pippin is badly hurt though. He needs help now.'

Then Cindy let out a primal roar of hatred and anger as she jumped back onto her feet. She had the knife in her hand, still red with Pippin's blood. My heart leapt into my mouth again just as I felt Jermaine react. He took a powerful step forward, pushing by me and shoving me backward toward the door and the concept of safety, but he didn't reach Cindy. He didn't need to. Barbie spun on her left foot, lifting the right so it prescribed a wide arc that ended when it connected with Cindy's nose. A perfect roundhouse kick.

'That's for calling me a slut!' she yelled, all pumped up with adrenalin and bouncing on the spot. Cindy's head had snapped back from the blow and the knife flew from her hand as she collapsed unconscious to the floor. 'I didn't even get to sleep with him,' Barbie yelled, her naked boobs bouncing as she danced excitedly on the balls of her feet.

Jermaine and I stared for a second, our eyes flicking disbelievingly between Barbie and Cindy. She shrugged and grinned, then said, 'Boxercise classes.' As if that told us everything we needed to know.

Unsure what to think of all the madness, the one thing I knew was that Pippin needed help. 'Jermaine, could you get some medical assistance for Pippin now, please?'

He said, 'Yes, madam,' and vanished back into the living area to make a call.

I started across the room to check on Pippin, just as Barbie went to him as well. I had to step around the foetal form of Shane to get there. 'Shane?' I called, remembering the shot he had charged down. 'Are you hurt?'

'Yeah,' he groaned. 'My nuts are killing me.'

'Are you shot?' I asked him as I knelt down next to Barbie, my focus on the blood-soaked form at my feet.

'He's still alive,' she told me, her finger on his neck to feel his pulse. 'He's lost a lot of blood though.'

Just then he opened his eyes. They flickered a few times but he looked up and proved that he probably wasn't as bad as I feared because he was staring directly at Barbie's chest. Admittedly there is a lot of it to look at and her boobs were hanging right over his face as she checked him, but if he had enough blood left in him to divert some of it to the growing lump in his trousers, then he probably wasn't about to die.

Behind me, Shane had struggled to his feet and was checking himself for bullet holes. He found one in the frilly bit of his naughty maid outfit and was poking a finger through it curiously. 'It went right through,' he said when he saw me looking and turned so I could see. Through blind luck the bullet had missed his body completely. Pippin was alive, Shane was unhurt, Barbie had survived yet another attack and the woman trying to kill her was the last person I would have suspected. It was a lot to take in. I leaned forward to whisper to Barbie that she might want to find a dressing gown or something to cover herself, then stayed with Pippin as she rooted in her wardrobe to find a grey flannel warm-up suit. It covered her though she had dressed quickly and skipped putting on a bra so her nipples were poking through the material for all to see.

A commotion outside was quickly revealed to be the guard arriving. Less than a minute later a pair of paramedics ran into the room. Followed a few seconds later by Mr Ikari.

When they had the now conscious Cindy in cuffs, Mr Ikari asked what had happened. 'He saved my life,' replied Barbie before I could speak. She was looking at Pippin as she said it. 'Jermaine went out to collect fresh provisions for tonight's dinner and there was a knock on the door just a few seconds later. Pippin opened it and she stabbed him and forced her way in. I was getting changed at the time, but I heard him yell and went to see what was happening just as she burst into my bedroom. He was wrestling her for the knife, but she got his gun and started yelling at me for stealing Tarquin and stealing her role. At least we know who killed Tarquin now and why.'

I was sure I should be feeling relief, but all I really felt was exhausted. The adrenalin had drained away, leaving me tired and wanting to curl up on the bed. Barbie and I were both sitting at the end of it while we watched the EMTs deal with Pippin. They had stripped back his clothing and quickly dressed the wound. One commented that his artery must be nicked but not severed or he would have already bled to death. An IV of plasma was running into his right arm but it was too soon for his colour to return. He would be taken away on a gurney soon enough and we would keep him company until then.

Jermaine brought refreshments because that was what Jermaine did. From somewhere, his expert fingers had produced a spread of crustless, delicate sandwiches and bite sized cakes plus tea with enough cups to serve everyone. I considered going to get changed. I was still wearing the ridiculous naughty maid outfit but I was so battered by the events of the day that my embarrassment over hanging out of it no longer felt all that big of a concern.

A few minutes later, as they were preparing to lift Pippin onto the stretcher to take him out, Barbie leaned into me and said, 'Is it okay if I move out now that all this madness is finished?'

'Goodness, yes, of course,' I replied. 'Whatever you need to do, sweetie.'

She nodded wistfully. 'It's been an odd couple of days. I think I might go for a workout and then come back to get my things. Do you want to come with me? It might take our minds off things.'

Sensing that she needed something to distract herself with, I said, 'Sure. That sounds like a great idea.' It really didn't but when in doubt, Barbie always went to the gym and I would go with her because it would give Jermaine the chance to get a cleaning crew into the suite.

As we stood up to give the medics manoeuvring room, I spotted Shane lingering by the door. The mystery of Tarquin's killer was solved and now he had nowhere to go. I knew he had no friends among the film crew and couldn't help myself from feeling sorry for him. 'Shane will you join me for dinner tonight?' I asked. His face lit up at the invite. 'I want to hear all about how you used to be famous as a child.'

'Oh, I was just making that up,' he said, sounding disappointed. 'Trying to talk her down by sounding like I knew what she was going through.'

I chuckled at him. 'Well, it was very well acted. I was utterly convinced. Maybe you should think about going on the stage yourself.' My compliment elicited a smile from him, and I touched my hand to his arm tactilely as I went out of the room. 'You were very brave, by the way. Charging at Cindy like that with no thought for your own safety.' He nodded but didn't speak, perhaps unable to think of a response that would suit the situation. 'Get cleaned up if you like, but come back for dinner and cocktails later, yes.'

'Thank you, Mrs Fisher. That sounds lovely.' I left him then, walking out of the bedroom with Barbie's arm looped through mine. My suite was still half full of people, but I knew they would clear out soon. Tarquin's killer had been caught and everyone I cared about was safe. Pippin would recover, or at least I certainly hoped he would, and I had to hope that his actions today would mean that the incident with Ian Kenyon would be overlooked.

In two days, we would dock in Hawaii and this would all be behind me. The film crew including Shane would depart and life on board would return to normal.

So why was there an itch at the back of my head telling me there was something amiss?

Incongruities

The sense that I had missed something or that something had been missed stayed with me for the rest of the afternoon. It was utterly intangible though, I could not put my finger on what it was that bothered me and though I kept telling myself to forget it, my brain found its way back to the question every time.

In the gym, Barbie performed a CrossFit routine of spin-bike, burpees, static jumps, and handstand pushups that would have crippled most people and then she attacked the weights like she had a personal vendetta against them. I stayed with her, doing my own slower version with simpler exercises for just over an hour before I called it quits. It was clear to me that she intended to keep pounding herself until the horror of the last few days went away, but if I pushed myself any longer, I would pay for it too dearly the next day.

I wished her luck and left her to it.

Despite the feeling of disquiet ticking away at the back of my head, nothing happened to me on my way back to my suite. I swiped my keycard against the reader to let myself in, instantly picking up the joyous scents of cooking coming from the open plan kitchen on the other side of my living area as I went inside. The bloody handprint on the doorframe in the lobby was gone, as was the blood that had fallen into the carpet. I didn't know what equipment they had to perform such tasks so quickly, but I was very impressed.

Suddenly hungry, I crossed the room to see what Jermaine was preparing. 'What've you got there Jermaine?' I asked, sniffing deeply.

'Madam I know how much of a fan you are of fish and how ready you are to try new cuisines.' He was right about that. This trip had been an

139

exploration for my taste buds. There were new foods I had never heard of at every destination the Aurelia took me to, and Jermaine had proved himself to be very knowledgeable about them all. 'So, I have prepared some Hawaiian dishes in celebration of your imminent first visit there,' he finished.

'Ooh, how exciting,' I gushed. 'What are we having?'

On the other side of the kitchen counter, Jermaine was expertly slicing raw vegetables with a large kitchen knife. He placed it to one side so he could look at me. 'As an appetiser I am making poke which is a raw fish dish much like sushi. This is aku poke which is made from yellowfin tuna. The fish, once prepared, is served with salt, seaweed and roasted, ground kukui nut meat. I am following that with Luau stew which is a comfort food dish made with beef brisket. It is quite spicy so I have already made,' he crossed to the refrigerator and opened the door to show me what was inside, 'some strawberry mochi which is actually a Japanese dish but can be found all over Hawaii.'

'They look like rice cakes,' I observed peering at the tray he was showing me.

'Yes, madam. That is what they are, but I believe you will be very pleased with them.' Jermaine was smiling, enjoying his task. 'Would you like to try the poke now?' he asked.

My eyes lit up as I tracked him back to the counter and the board he was preparing food on. He scooped ingredients into a tiny bowl no bigger than a ramekin and handed it to me along with a pair of chopsticks. I can report that it tasted heavenly. Fresh and delicate plus melt in the mouth tender. I had missed out on a lot in my first fifty years. Not for the first time, as I polished off the taster Jermaine gave me, I made a promise that the rest of my life was going to be different.

I handed the little dish back, saying, 'Thank you Jermaine.'

'You are very welcome, madam.'

'I am going to get changed, but then I am going out for a short while, there is something I wish to check on. If Barbie returns while I am out, please let her know that I will not be long.'

'Very good, madam.'

I took myself for a shower and dressed in a long, floating summer dress, then added a thin woollen cardigan as it was still cool though the worst of the storm had never arrived and there was no sign of rain outside. The thing that was bothering me still wouldn't surface, so I was going to ignore it for a while and visit Mr Ikari. There were always security officers near the upper deck restaurant. They would be able to contact him and give me his location. I wanted to know if Cindy had confessed to Tarquin's murder. I thought she had when she was in Barbie's bedroom, but thinking back, what she actually said was that he deserved to die for what he did to her. It might seem like semantics, but it wasn't a confession.

Coming out of my bedroom, Jermaine was on the suite's phone, the handset gripped delicately in his meaty right hand and held close to his ear but not touching it as if he didn't want to get it dirty. I was curious about who he might be talking to, but not rude enough to ask. He locked eyes with me though, suggesting that the call was for me.

'One moment, sir. I will need a moment to see if the lady is in.' Then he brought the handset away from his face and placed his other hand over the mouthpieces to muffle any noise at this end. 'Madam, the caller says his name is Charlie. He insists that he is your husband and has been trying to get hold of you for days.'

141

The news caught me completely off guard. Charlie knew where I was and had tracked down a way to call me on the ship. I knew the calls were possible, all it took was a little satellite technology, but I hadn't expected to hear from him.

'Shall I say you are not available, madam?' asked Jermaine, still holding the phone. My honest reaction was that I did not wish to speak to him, but I had a couple of elderly aunts back in England so he could be calling me with genuine news that I would need to hear.

Resigned to the task, I crossed the room and held out my hand. Jermaine brought the phone back up to his ear, saying, 'One moment, sir.' Then he handed it to me, giving the mouthpiece a quick wipe with a cloth he always kept handy.

Picking up the phone, I thought about what I wanted to say to him, but in the end, I settled with a simple, 'Hello, Charlie.'

'Patricia,' he started, his tone immediately impatient. 'Patricia, why haven't you been returning my calls? I have been trying to get hold of you for days.'

'My phone went in the pool, Charlie. I had to get a new one,' I replied. I could feel my ire rising. He was talking to me as if I was still his mousy, obedient housewife. As if nothing had changed. Maybe for him nothing much had changed, but life was very different for me. Not just because of my palatial surroundings, but because I looked at the world in a different way now. The last month had changed me.

Charlie wasn't satisfied by my answer though. 'Then why didn't you give me your new number?' he demanded.

I laughed at him. 'Why on earth would I do that?'

My answer caught him off guard. 'Well... well, because we are still married, that's why,' he argued.

'Only on paper, Charlie.'

'What do you mean?'

Right there in that very moment my decision was made. I didn't have to add up the pros and cons. I didn't need to weigh up the future. I knew what I wanted. 'I'll be filing for divorce when I get back, Charlie.'

'The hell you will,' he snapped.

'Why did you call, Charlie?' I asked to deflect him. I wanted to end the call as quickly as possible, but I wouldn't hang up the phone and let him make me the bad guy. If he had news about my family or something else important then I would listen, and I would thank him for it.

'I wanted to hear your voice,' he said, suddenly sounding meek. 'I miss you.'

'What about Maggie?' I asked, cruelly twisting the knife because I felt like I hadn't been allowed to do so anywhere near enough yet.

'That was a silly mistake, Patricia. It won't happen again.'

I had half expected this from him. He had never been good at apologising or taking the blame. Oh, he would say sorry if he forgot to take the trash out in time for the bin men to collect it or went to the shop but forgot to pick up the thing that I asked him to get. But, if he had really messed up, like the year he forgot my birthday, he always had excuses why and managed to make it my fault somehow.

'Tell me, Charlie. Exactly how many times did that mistake happen over how many years?' There was no answer from the other end. 'No answer?' I prompted.

'This is not all my fault, Patricia,' he started. But I cut over him.

'Don't even bother trying to deflect this onto me, Charles Fisher,' I raged. 'I have no interest in listening to your apologies, let alone your excuses. Do you have anything you need to talk to me about other than the end of our marriage?'

'Where are you, Snookums?' he asked, using a pet name for me that he probably hadn't uttered in over five years. There was a time, many years ago, when he could turn my legs to jelly using that name and the right tone of voice. Today it made me want to gag.

'We dock in Hawaii in two days,' I said to get to the end of the call and get rid of him.

'Hawaii? I'll see you there.' Then he was gone, leaving nothing but a dial tone sounding in my ear.

I said, 'Hello? Charlie, hello?' He had hung up before I could argue. Charlie wouldn't be in Hawaii in two days. Charlie never went anywhere. That was what I told myself as a sliver of dread crept though me. Then a little voice reminded me that he had made his way to St Kitts to meet me there. Surely Hawaii was too far to come though.

'Is everything alright, madam?' asked Jermiane.

I still had the phone in my hand, staring at it brainlessly as if trying to work what I was supposed to do with it next. I was still doing the maths in my head, but I decided it was nothing more than an idle threat from a man too used to having the upper hand. I would start divorce proceedings

144

when I returned to England in eight weeks' time. It would take a while, but I had money of my own to keep me going and I was quietly confident that the divorce settlement would provide sufficient funds to buy myself a nice cottage. Maybe I would get a dog.

I replaced the handset, shooting a smile at Jermaine. 'Just peachy, Jermaine. Nothing to be concerned about.'

'Very good, madam. Um, Madam?'

'Yes.'

'If you ever need anything...'

Jermaine was being supportive. He was far more than just my butler during my stay on the ship. He was my friend and I hoped he knew that was how I felt. I offered him a warm smile. 'Thank you, Jermaine.'

Barbie still hadn't returned to get her clothes and other personal items, but I didn't go to the gym to see if she was okay. The threat against her was gone and it might be best for people to leave her to settle back into her usual routine instead of constantly worrying and checking on her. I went right by the gym door on my way to the upper deck restaurant where I found, just as I had expected, two security guards. One of them was Schneider, a tall Austrian I got to know quite well when he was acting as my personal bodyguard a short while ago. He spotted me and waved. Next to him was Lieutenant Bhukari from earlier.

The guards used the restaurant as a convenient place to hang out when meals were not being served. Not that they slouched about and were skiving. It was just a place to stay out of the heat for a few minutes and it was very centrally located should they need to react to anything.

Schneider reached out to shake my hand. 'Mrs Fisher, I heard about the excitement in your suite. Are you quite alright?' He asked.

'Yes, thank you. The last couple of days have been rather adventurous,' I admitted with a tinge of humour as I smiled at his female colleague. She smiled back but didn't say anything about taking me into custody earlier. Then I asked them both, 'Can you locate Mr Ikari for me, please? I have a question to ask him.'

Schneider nodded and leaned his face down to speak into his microphone. Mr Ikari's voice was recognisable despite the tinny sound the radio added. 'I have Mrs Fisher with me, sir. She has a question for you. Over'

There was a pause while he considered what to do. 'I cannot leave the bridge currently. Would Mrs Fisher like to come to me? Over.'

'Yes, that's fine.' I answered Schneider's questioning expression.

He replayed the message to Mr Ikari, who replied with, 'If you are coming now, please let Mrs Fisher know that there may be a slight wait. The captain and I have matters to discuss but I will not keep her long. Out.'

At the mention of the captain my stomach gave another little flutter and my brain supplied me with a memory of his warm hand on mine. I shoved the memory back down, not wanting to dwell on it. I was still married, even if I had moved on emotionally, and I wasn't going to fool myself that the captain was genuinely interested in me. I was a frumpy, middle-aged lady. I might have been a catch once, but those years were behind me.

Bringing myself under control, I said, 'Lead on,' to Schneider and Bhukari and followed them from the room. Access to the bridge wasn't far

146

from the upper deck restaurant so it didn't take long to reach the crew-only elevator. Unlike the other crew elevators this one could only be called by use of a keypad. Schneider wisely shielded the code from me using his body when he entered it, the doors swishing instantly open to reveal the car already on our deck and waiting.

'After you, Mrs Fisher,' said Bhukari politely as all three of us got in and we remained silent as the box hummed quietly on its journey up.

Mr Ikari was waiting for me when the doors opened, dismissing my two escorts to go back to their duties as he led me away from the elevator. The doors hadn't opened onto the bridge itself as I had imagined. Instead, I was in a corridor that had many rooms coming off from it. Thinking about it for the first time, the superstructure that led up to the bridge was enormous so it should have been obvious that there wasn't one really big room at the top. Had I expected a really big steering wheel too?

As we walked, Mr Ikari explained why it was that I didn't have to wait after all. 'The captain said we could delay our meeting until after your visit. He seemed keen to allow you access to the bridge. Very few passengers get to come up here. This is a special privilege indeed.'

I didn't know what to make of that news, so I smiled rather than say anything but then thought I should ask my question since I was already here. 'Mr Ikari, I wanted to ask about the woman that attacked Barbie.'

'Cindy Telford? What about her?'

'Has she confessed to killing Tarquin Trebeck?' I asked. It was a direct question with a yes or no answer. I didn't get an answer though; I got a question.

'Why do you ask, Mrs Fisher?' He paused at that point and turned to face me.

I blew out a breath as I searched for a good answer to his question. 'Because... because something doesn't quite fit.'

'What, Mrs Fisher? What is it that doesn't fit?' He sounded truly curious to hear what I had to say.

'I'm not sure,' I stuttered. 'I don't seem to be able to quite work it out. Has she confessed?' I asked again.

Mr Ikari pursed his lips in frustration. 'No, she hasn't. In fact, she is adamant that she had nothing to do with it. She doesn't have an alibi for the night of his murder, claiming to have taken painkillers for the broken ankle and gone to bed early.'

'Do you believe her?' I asked, searching his face to see if the facial cues would match his answer.

He thought for a second but as he opened his mouth to answer, his radio squawked. The voice coming over the airwave said, 'Secretary, secretary, secretary. Cumberland suite. I repeat; Cumberland suite. Out.'

Mr Ikari's eyes were as wide as they could go. I took the message to be code of some sort, but I didn't know what for. Then I frowned. 'Wait a second; the Cumberland suite, that's...'

'Ian Kenyon's cabin,' he said as he took my elbow and started moving me back toward the elevator. 'I have only heard the code word secretary twice in my entire career.'

'What does it mean?' I asked, letting him pull me along and desperate to know what was happening.

He punched numbers into the keypad to summon the elevator and sighed as he said, 'The codeword secretary means a passenger has been found dead.'

As my hand shot to my mouth, the doors to the elevator swished open. I got in with Mr Ikari but he shoved his foot into the closing door when someone bellowed, 'Hold the door!'

The doors fought against him for a moment and then reopened revealing half a dozen white uniforms running toward us. At the head was the captain himself. 'Mrs Fisher,' he nodded as he darted to my side to let the rest of his men get in. Facing forward to look at the closed doors, he addressed his number two, 'Mr Ikari, I feel this is becoming a habit.'

'Murders you mean?' I asked.

'No one said murder,' Mr Ikari pointed out. It was a valid point, but I was willing to bet money that someone had found Ian Kenyon dead in his cabin and it wasn't going to be a heart attack. We all spilled from the elevator the moment the doors began to open, the men and one woman in white uniforms breaking into a fast jog and calling ahead to clear passengers out of their way. I had to run to keep up and I had on summer slip-on shoes that were not designed for running. I stopped to slip them off, the female guard turning to check on me, but I waved for her to keep going as I restarted running in bare feet.

The fast-moving contingent of white uniforms drew a lot of stares from passengers tucked into the sides of the passageways as did I as I ran along twenty feet behind them to make it look like I were giving chase and they were trying to get away from me. My treacherous brain supplied a snippet of Benny Hill chase music though there was nothing funny about this situation at all.

We reached the passageway that led to Ian Kenyon's suite to find it had already been emptied of passengers. The ship's security were visible at the far end, stopping anyone from coming this way and also at the end we entered from. I was the only person inside the cordon that wasn't in a white uniform. The door to Ian's suite was open and Schneider was standing outside of it, conversing with the captain and Mr Ikari when I caught up to them. I peered inside but could not see anything and could not get inside because of the men blocking the way.

It was only when my forward progress was stopped by a barrier, that I questioned what it was that I thought I was doing. Why was I even here? I could hear Schneider telling the senior officers that Paul Deacon, who was staying in a suite two doors along, had called to see if Ian wanted to get dinner, found the door open and discovered his body laying behind the sofa. 'It looks like he was strangled,' said Schneider.

It was then that it struck me. The thing that had been itching away at the back of my head. When Cindy came to my suite and tried to kill Barbie, we had all assumed that she had already killed Tarquin for dumping her. She was a tiny little thing though not possessing the strength required to subdue him and cut his throat. The killer had to be a man. That Ian had been killed while Cindy was in custody was just further proof that the killer was still at large.

From the far end of the corridor, I could see a person I recognised from the ship's medical team. She was one of the doctors, undoubtedly summoned to pronounce death. As she hurried toward us, Schneider stepped to one side to let the captain and Mr Ikari enter Ian's cabin. No one barred my way, so I followed the others into the room. I was getting used to seeing bodies, I had actually lost count of how many it now was, but I could add Ian Kenyon to my growing list.

He looked strangely peaceful though his head was at a slightly unnatural angle. He still wore his glasses and he was fully dressed. Laying on the carpet next to his couch as if he had fallen asleep and rolled off without waking up. His neck bore traces of a fight, slight bruising that would fail to develop fully because his blood was no longer flowing.

'Just how many killers have we currently got on board, Mr Ikari?' asked the captain wistfully. It was a rhetorical question but a good one because they had only taken the murderous Cindy into custody a few hours ago and they clearly still had someone with a grudge.

'Where is Bhavana?' I asked.

'Her current whereabouts are being investigated,' replied Mr Ikari. 'I'm afraid, Mrs Fisher, that I will have to ask one of the men to escort you back outside the cordon.' He held up an apologetic hand. 'I know you have been heavily involved and may thus feel quite invested in the outcome of this murder enquiry, but...'

I held up my own hand to stop him. 'It's perfectly alright, Mr Ikari. I have no place here. If you will excuse me, I will take myself back to my suite. I have had quite the day.' My shoes were still in my hand, so I dropped them lightly to the carpet, then accepted the captain's hand as he moved to offer it as balance while I slipped my feet into them. Then said, 'Thank you, Captain,' as he let me go again.

He held my gaze though as he said, 'You are most welcome, Mrs Fisher.' A beat passed before we broke the gaze and feeling warmth on my cheeks, I bid the other occupants good day and left them to it.

Walking back along the passageway toward the cordon, I was still running through the puzzle pieces in my head. Ian hadn't been the killer, I knew that for certain, and he certainly hadn't killed himself. So, if I was right to assume that Cindy also wasn't Tarquin's killer, even though she would have gleefully dispatched Barbie, then I was still stuck with trying to work out who was.

It wasn't so much that I thought Mr Ikari wasn't up to the job, but more that I felt this was all just a little bit too close to me. The thing that had been itching away at the back of my head wasn't Cindy's insufficient strength to kill Tarquin, it was something else.

So, while Mr Ikari had his guards look for Bhavana, the one person that stuck out as having potential motive, I was going back to my suite to conduct some research.

Shane had been good enough to supply us with the lead that made us look at Ian Kenyon. It had proved to be solid information even though it eventually proved to be erroneous as a potential motive. I took his advice at face value when he presented it and was only now wondering why I hadn't taken the time to check it for myself. What else might I have found out if I had looked?

Jermaine was not in sight when I got back to my suite. But I had no need to summon him and in fact felt glad that he was probably in his suite resting and relaxing for once. I was getting hungry, but he would serve food as soon as I asked, and no doubt Shane would be along soon.

I kicked off my shoes again, strolled through to the kitchen to fetch myself a glass of cold water and settled in front of the computer. As it booted into life, I thought about what it was I wanted to look up. Ian Kenyon probably had enemies, goodness knows he was an irritable little man, but if I assumed the killer was someone from the film industry in which he worked then it was going to be one of the film crew that had come on board with him. I would start doing some research and have Shane check the list to see if there were any names he recognised.

It was easy to find Tarquin and his early career. There was an IMDB for him that listed all his films in order. *Summer Adventure* was right there at the top, the familiar poster displayed next to the cast list and other details. I dismissed that search though and brought up Ian Kenyon. There was a series of headshots and a career biography, but I couldn't find the pages that Shane had read. There was no information I could find about who he had signed when he was an agent and certainly no details about the incident with Tarquin's mother. No doubt it was here somewhere, and I just wasn't putting in the right search terms.

Just then, I heard the adjoining door open from Jermaine's cabin. As I glanced across at the door, he came through it, wearing his full butler's outfit complete with tails. 'Good evening, madam. May I bring you a beverage?'

It was a question which interested me. I had invited Shane to come for dinner and cocktails, but I could start without him. 'Perhaps just a small gin and tonic?'

'Yes, madam. The Hendricks?' he asked, holding the bottle up for me to see. It was certainly my favourite.

I nodded and offered a thumbs up then turned back to my screen. Failing to find anything of use of Ian Kenyon, I minimised that window and started a new search, this time looking at Bhavana. Had she somehow found out about Ian's plans with the FBI? They were waiting to swoop but as I understood it, they had no jurisdiction in international water or on board this boat, but the second we docked in Hawaii, they would be back on American soil and could make the arrest if they felt they had enough evidence. The evidence they had been after though was Bhavana blackmailing Ian. They hadn't been able to record her threats when I overheard her and now there would be no threats. Was the case against her about to fall apart?

Looking at her history online didn't reveal anything I found useful, neither did the search through her past films and list of other actors she had starred alongside. Jermaine arrived with my balloon glass of gin, settling it on a coaster and turning it so it sat just right. 'Do you have time to help me?' I asked as he straightened up.

'Madam, my time is yours. What is it that I can do for you?' he replied.

I realised then that he probably didn't know about Ian Kenyon. But another thought took precedence. 'Did Barbie return for her clothes?' I asked, suddenly worried.

'Yes, madam. Miss Berkeley collected her belongings just moments after you departed.' She must have exited the gym just seconds after I passed it. I told him about Ian Kenyon's murder and that the person that killed Tarquin Trebeck was probably still at large.

He took the news calmly, but then asked, 'Would you mind if I made a phone call, madam. I believe I would sleep less fitfully if I knew Miss Berkeley to be safe.'

'Of course,' I replied, going back to the screen while Jermaine called Barbie. I felt it unlikely that Barbie was is in any danger. The person that killed Tarquin was probably the same person that had killed Ian and the attacks upon Barbie had all been perpetrated by Cindy. Nevertheless, I was thankful to have him check on her.

Getting nowhere with my searches, I waited for Jermaine to finish his call and come back to me. The brief pause gave me the chance to sip my gin and tonic. As expected, he had translated my request for just a little one into a strong double. If I was going to drink gin, I intended to taste it.

Jermaine ended the call and slipped his mobile back into a pocket. 'Now then, madam, what is it that I can assist you with?' he asked.

I pointed to the screen. 'You remember Shane explaining about Tarquin's history with Ian?'

'Yes, madam.'

'Well, I am struggling to find that information. I want to dive a little deeper and see who else might have held a grudge against either of them, or maybe find something that connects the pair of them to someone else. I think I need a little help though.' When I finished explaining what I had found so far, Jermaine pulled up a chair next to me and sat down.

'This might take a while, madam, so perhaps, to be thorough, we should go back to the start of their careers and work from there.' Jermaine suggested, taking the mouse and clicking it to bring up Tarquin's IMDB again.

I said, 'Sure. My working premise is that those two have been targeted by one person because of a connection with a third person. But Ian and Tarquin only worked together for a brief period at the very start of his career. The alternate theory is that Tarquin and Ian were killed by separate people for separate reasons. If that is the case, then this will be much harder, if not impossible to work out.' My thoughts went to Bhavana again, but I knew she hadn't killed Tarquin because she was with Ian when that happened.

Jermaine clicked into *Summer Adventure*, the poster displaying on the screen once more. Little Tarquin, playing younger brother to the star of the show was there as always, almost forgotten at the very edge of the picture which was dominated by the older boy in the middle. Looking at him again now, I thought there was something familiar about him. His eyes maybe. Jermaine clicked the mouse again, taking him back off the page to the list of actors before I could ask him about it and I dismissed the notion. Looking now at the list of other actors in that first film, Jermaine explained that each one could be searched to see what else they had done. There was potential to create millions of different connections.

I pointed to the screen just as Jermaine was about to click on Tarquin's picture. 'Take us into that kid. The one who had the lead in the film. Barbie said his career stalled after this film. Who is he even?' The name below the picture was Jeremiah Anthony Bumblethorpe; I had never heard of him. Staring so intently at the screen, I jumped when someone knocked on the door. Jermaine went to answer it, but we were expecting Shane, so it was no surprise when I saw him coming through the door. He had on casual clothes for dinner, jeans and running shoes with a hoody his hands were stuffed into.

'Would you care for a drink, sir?' asked Jermaine, closing the door and passing Shane as he made his way to the kitchen.

'No thank you,' Shane replied. 'Actually, I just popped by to say that I am not feeling well and think I should take myself to bed.'

I turned my head to look at the young man. 'Oh, you poor, love. This really had been a trying trip for you, hasn't it?' Jermaine made no comment about the dinner he had made going to ruin and returned to his seat next to me.

He nodded but then looked at the screen behind me. I turned around to see what he was looking at. 'Oh, yes, we are just looking into connections between Tarquin and Ian and anyone else that might link the two to a third person.

You shouldn't have done that,' Shane said, his voice dripping with disappointment.

I started to say, 'Why ever not...' but the sentence trailed off without finishing because Jermaine had clicked the mouse to bring up more details about Jeremiah. On the first line of his bio was his real name.

Jermaine stared at it, then a smile flickered across his face as he said, 'Hold on. That's you.' He pointed at the screen and turned his head to look back at Shane.

Shane hit him across the back of his head with a heavy candlestick, the sickening thump it produced telling me how much force he had put into it. I leaped away from him, diving out of my seat to get some distance but he didn't follow me.

'You're going to ask me why, aren't you?' he stated, taking a step forward to check Jermaine wasn't going to get up. My butler was lying face down on the desk, a trickle of bright red blood coming from a lump just behind his ear. Shane took a moment to look at the screen, tutting as he stabbed the power button to shut it off. I had seen the evidence though. Jeremiah Anthony Bumblethorpe was a stage name. The boy actor's real name was Shane Sussmann and now that I knew what to look for, I could see the resemblance.

I hadn't replied to his statement. I hadn't asked him why, but I could tell he was going to tell me anyway. As I cowered on the floor, wondering how I could possibly escape and whether Jermaine was okay, the short, plump man settled into the seat I had just vacated. 'I was the big star,' he said, a faraway look in his eyes as he stared not at me but at some point in the past. 'My future was all mapped out. I knew exactly what sort of films I was going to star in: avoid sequels, keep pushing myself to take on challenging roles that would stretch me as an actor. I had already been in six movies when I was cast as the lead in *Summer Adventure*, Tarquin was just some kid they brought in at the last minute to play my little brother. I remember the day Ian brought him to set. We were already filming, and he looked so nervous. He was just a couple of years younger than me, but I took him under my wing, made sure he knew his lines and taught him all kinds of stuff. The film wrapped as they always do, and I moved onto the next project. But the film I was supposed to be making got shelved and Ian didn't have another role for me. He kept saying not to worry and that something would come up soon. He said he was holding out for the right role like we had talked about. I wanted to go for a film called *On falcon Rock* but he said it wasn't right for me.'

Next to him, Jermaine groaned. Shane picked up the brass candlestick again, hefting high above his head. I started to get to my feet; I had to stop him, but when Jermaine didn't make any further noise, Shane put it down again and started talking once more.

'Ian didn't think the role was right for me because he was pushing Tarquin for it. When he landed it, I got a letter from a lawyer to let me know that I had been dropped from his agency. Just like that. I tried getting another agent but I was a child star that was no longer really a child and where I had been tall for an eleven year old, I stopped growing at twelve and then in my depression I put on a few pounds and no one would give me a role. I was always too well known or not quite what they were looking for or I was known for a different kind of role. I always believed I could work my way back into it somehow, so I took jobs on film sets doing lighting and pyrotechnics. I was even a runner for a while. Do you have any idea how menial and low that task is?' he asked.

I shook my head.

'Over the years I learned to live with it. At least I thought I had. After a few years I accepted that I wasn't going to have a big career in Hollywood and would have to settle for the jobs I could get. I was still working in the movies, right?' he said brightly, a smile forced onto his grim face. 'Then the effects company I work for got this gig and it sounded like a sweet deal. Filming on board a luxury cruise ship and then Hawaii? I was on board before I heard that Tarquin Trebeck was the lead actor. I honestly considered quitting but then he would have really won the final victory, so I bit down on my envy and anger and went to see him. You know; to shake his hand for old times' sake. He said he didn't know who I was. I called him a liar and he hit me. I couldn't even hit him back because his body

160

double stepped in to block me and I got hauled away by a load of stagehands. That was when I saw Ian Kenyon. As the producer, it was his job to fire me, but he took pity and kept me on. Took pity. Can you believe that? I wanted to kill him, and in that moment, I knew I would never be able to rest until I got my own back.'

'So, what now?' I asked quietly, terrified for what his answer might be.

He sniffed and looked at the floor when he answered, unwilling to look directly at me. 'Now I have to clean up some loose ends.'

'You don't have to, Shane. You can just…'

'What?' he snapped, looking into my eyes now. 'Let you go. Keep you in here until we get to Hawaii and then escape and hope you won't turn me in? I didn't want any of this. I wanted Ian Kenyon framed for Tarquin's murder. Nice, neat, easy. Then that crazy Cindy Telford came after Barbie and everyone started looking into things they didn't need to look into.' He seemed genuinely upset about his plan to kill me.

He looked about the room, his eyes settling on the glass doors that led out to the private sun terrace. Then he got to his feet and hooked his arms under Jermaine's shoulders to try lifting him. He struggled for a few seconds before accepting that he was too heavy. Then, as he settled him back into his chair, he said, 'I'm going to need you to give me a hand with him. He's a bit heavy.'

'A hand?' I asked, confused. 'Where are you trying to take him?'

He frowned as if it was a daft question. 'Outside. I'm going to toss him overboard.'

'Oh no you're not!' I yelled my challenge as I lunged for the candlestick and grabbed it before he could. I hefted it above my head like a bat, but

161

Shane showed no sign of fear. Instead, he reached inside the pouch of his hoody and pulled out a small axe.

'Have you ever watched *Summer Adventure*?' he asked calmly, his eyebrows raised as he waited to hear my reply. 'It's really not a bad movie. They taught me to throw an axe and I have never forgotten how to do it. This is the one from the film, in fact.' While he talked about the weapon, he was fingering it lovingly and staring down at it as if he were talking to it and not me. His eyes snapped back up now though. 'Put the candlestick down,' he growled.

I was utterly gripped by terror. Shane was going to kill me and kill Jermaine and maybe once he had, no one would ever work out who had killed us or Tarquin or Ian.

'I said, put it down,' he growled again, louder this time to break me from my petrified state. I let it tumble from my fingers to fall on the floor with a thump.

Then a knock at the door startled both of us and our eyes locked for a nanosecond before I seized my one chance and screamed for help. Shane lunged for me, wrapping me into a hug as he tried to smother my mouth. I had no idea who was outside but anyone hearing my banshee wail to be saved would at least have the sense to fetch help. I hoped.

I fought against Shane, but he was strong as an ox, lifting me off my feet so I couldn't get any purchase on the carpet. Then he threw me to one side as a new shout filled the air. There were men in white uniforms coming through my door.

I bounced painfully on the floor, feeling the skin on my elbow tear but I was the right way up to see Shane pull back his arm and throw the axe. As it sailed through the air, tumbling end over end, I heard a gunshot, followed quickly by two more. The guards were shooting at Shane but all I could watch was the axe.

It struck home, the head vanishing into Mr Ikari's chest just above his heart as he rushed into the room with his gun up. He had led the charge, the brave leader running ahead of his team as they faced unknown dangers.

A thumping crash on the carpet next to me told me Shane was down but yet again I was too stunned to move. Instantly, the room was filled with the shouts of the security team, some running forward to make sure the threat was isolated, others immediately switching their attention to the wounded Mr Ikari.

In something of a daze, and largely ignored by those around me, I staggered to my feet, stumbling as they refused to obey my commands. I crossed the short space to where Jermaine still lay with his head on the desk.

He was unconscious but breathing, the lump on the back of his head like a chicken's egg under the skin. The trickle of blood had all but stopped and he groaned again as I touched his shoulders.

'How bad is he?' asked a woman's voice. I turned to find Lieutenant Bhukari's concerned face leaning across the desk.

Jermaine chose that convenient moment to come around. 'Ow,' he said, squinting his eyes and feeling the back of his head as he started to sit up again.

From his position on the floor Lieutenant Baker asked, 'Who is this?'

I looked down at him, taking in the man lying on my carpet next to him. It was obvious to anyone that Shane was dead, his quest for revenge ultimately costing him his life. 'It's Jeremiah Anthony Bumblethorpe,' I said quietly.

'The kid from *Summer Adventure*?' he queried, staring down at the strange man in disbelief. That he had instantly recognised the name was so ridiculously ironic I almost laughed. What would Shane have made of it, I wondered.

Next to me, Lieutenant Bhukari was sniffing the air. 'Is something burning?' she asked.

'Dinner!' I squealed, remembering the stew still simmering on the hob. Jermaine stood up suddenly, on his way to deal with it, but had to grab the desk as wooziness gripped him. I said, 'Stay there. I've got it.' Leaving Lieutenant Bhukari to settle him back into his seat. Somehow, among all the madness, threat and death, I was in the kitchen dealing with a burnt dinner like it was a normal evening at home.

Less than a minute had passed since the guards burst into my room, but more people were already starting to arrive. The guards would have summoned additional officers, paramedics to deal with Mr Ikari's injury, a doctor to pronounce death and probably the captain. My hopeful thought that the captain might make an appearance made me blush and then berate myself for acting like a fool. I needed to dismiss any foolish romantic notions now before they became a distraction.

Calmly running the tap into the crispy black pan, I accepted that dinner was ruined. To be fair, my appetite had evaporated anyway. I slumped onto the kitchen counter, my head in my hands as I watched the organised pandemonium in front of me. Over the course of the next thirty minutes, Shane's body was removed, Mr Ikari was taken to the medical bay where the axe would be surgically removed. He wasn't in any danger, it seemed, but he would have to be transferred to hospital in Hawaii and would have a long recovery ahead of him. Jermaine was also taken to the medical bay though he protested until I insisted.

As the dozen or more people in my living space went about the tasks, I thought back to all the clues I had missed. Shane had fainted when he first saw blood, but earlier today, he overcame his aversion and remained calm in Barbie's bedroom with Pippin leaking all over the carpet. It was only now that I remembered him referring to Tarquin as a childhood friend earlier. It had happened when we were leaving Ian Kenyon's cabin escorted by Baker and Bhukari. It hadn't even registered at the time. I couldn't ask him about it, but I believed it had been a slip of the tongue that he kept quiet about while hoping no one had heard him. There were other clues too such as his convincing pretence that he had been famous once and was now forgotten. He hadn't been pretending at all and he knew all about Ian and Tarquin's history even though I could find no trace of it on the internet. Then there was possibly the biggest clue which was that Shane had known Tarquin's throat had been cut when it wasn't public knowledge. Looking back now, it should have been obvious he was up to something. I bowed my head with defeat and fatigue and stayed that way until I heard a familiar voice.

It came just as Mr Ikari was being stretchered out, the captain sweeping into the room and shaking the man's hand as he was taken away. He spoke to each of the officers and crew members in the room, thanking each for their efforts and he took several minutes with Lieutenant Deepa Bhukari, counselling her about the potential effects she could now experience. I learned that she had been credited with shooting Shane, though I doubted credited was the word she would want people to use. He insisted that she report to the medical bay to discuss emotional management. Then, having been working his way towards me, he finally arrived at the far side of the room where I was still slumped on the kitchen counter.

'Good evening, Mrs Fisher.' He offered me a smile but then fixed me with a serious look. 'Are you okay?'

I waved a hand in submission. 'It's nothing a stiff gin wouldn't fix.' I replied flippantly.

'Then I shall take great pleasure in fixing you one.' I cocked an eyebrow, but the captain was already moving, undoing his jacket as he came around the kitchen counter. I levered myself upright, surprised but not displeased by his proximity as he shuffled behind me to get to the glasses. 'Do you mind if I join you?' he asked, holding up two balloon glasses.

'Err, no. No, of course not,' I stuttered, and then watched as he pushed up his sleeves to reveal lean, muscular forearms and started pulling together ingredients.

'Do you know where Special Rating Clarke keeps the tonic?' he asked, not finding it in the refrigerator.

'There's an additional refrigerator under the counter for drinks,' I said, pointing to the fitted door that hid it.

While he busied himself making us two gin and tonics, he started up a conversation. 'I will, of course, appoint you a stand-in butler until yours can be cleared for duty.'

'No, please,' I begged. 'That will not be necessary. 'Honestly, I think I will enjoy fending for myself for a day or so.'

'I doubt it will be that long, but if you insist... You may be interested to know that I have appointed an interim deputy captain. Mr Ikari will need time to recover and will most likely be appointed to a different ship when he is recovered,' he explained.

'Who did you choose?' I asked since he hadn't said.

Finishing with a wedge of lime; I would have picked cucumber, but I wasn't going to comment, the handsome, debonair captain handed me my drink. Then said, 'Cheers,' as he clinked his glass against mine. After taking a sip, he answered my question. 'I don't get to pick, actually. Rank and seniority dictates who is next in line. The only position that cannot be automatically granted by being the next most senior person is captain. Anyway, Commander Farrokhzad is the next in line but he declined the opportunity so Commander Shriver is currently in the big chair on the bridge.'

'Did he say why he didn't want the job?' I asked.

The captain chuckled as he took a sip of his drink. 'Yes, he did. He said the job was cursed. In the last month alone Mr Schooner went to jail, Mr Rutherford was sacked and Mr Ikari is on his way to hospital.' Then he levelled his eyes at me. 'I probably shouldn't tell you this, but he said he would gladly take the job once you were no longer on board.' Then he laughed again as my jaw fell open in shock. 'He suggested a correlation between the recent... events and your presence here.'

'And what do you think?' I asked squinting my eyes at him as I heard the snippiness in my tone.

'I think you are lovely,' he replied. His response came back without hesitation, but I could see that he hadn't meant to say it. We looked at each other for a second, both wondering what the other might say next.

I chose to break the silence with a question of my own. Diverting attention away from the awkwardness we both felt. 'You were telling me about how a person cannot be promoted to captain just by being the next most senior person.' I asked genuinely interested to hear more about him.

He shot me a smile and leaned on the kitchen counter. He was facing me, so that our faces were no more than a foot apart across the expanse of marble. 'Well, Patricia.' It wasn't lost on me that it was the first time he had addressed me by my first name. 'It's like this...'

As the cleaners scrubbed blood from my carpet and repair men dealt with damage wrought during today's scuffle, Alistair Huntley told me all about how he came to be the captain of the Aurelia. It was perhaps, the most relaxed I had felt since I came on board. I had to wonder what was happening, but I had no intention of asking him why he seemed to enjoy my company. Instead, I listened and sipped my gin and began to worry that the trip would end too soon.

Just then the unpleasant little woman that ran Guest Services came into my suite. Marianne Redmond was there to supervise the cleaners and ensure their jobs were performed correctly. No doubt she attended herself because it was the Royal Suite, but as she checked on their progress and came toward the captain to report, she caught sight of me, her expression telling me she recognised me from our earlier interaction.

She levelled an excited arm at me as she speed-marched in my direction. The captain intercepted her though. 'Marianne, have you had the pleasure of meeting Mrs Fisher?' he asked.

The question stopped her dead in her tracks, her anger and desire to tear into a woman she believed to be an insolent staff member fizzing out instantly under the captain's gaze. 'Err, no. No, I haven't,' she said, trying to offer me a smile but failing badly as if she had read about them in books but never actually seen one before.

Then Alistair said something that rooted me to the spot almost as completely as Shane's earlier threat of death had, 'Mrs Fisher is with me.'

Post Script:

The following morning, the sky was clear once more and sun streamed through the curtains when I opened them. The scent of fresh coffee lifted me to full alertness as I opened my bedroom door to find a contented Jermaine in the kitchen, humming to himself with his back to me. He had a large white dressing on his head, held in place with a bandage but he was back in place as my butler and clearly happy to be here. I was happy too.

I called out, 'Good morning, Jermaine.'

He turned and gave a me a broad smile. 'Indeed, it is, madam. Will you be training this morning?' he asked, pouring me a cup of strong, dark liquid.

'You know, I think I will,' I replied. And I did, setting off to find Barbie in the gym less than thirty minutes later. I took my coffee onto the sun terrace first though, soaking up vitamin D from the sun and staring into the distance where Hawaii already loomed large. I was bothered by a niggling concern that Charlie might turn up though it seemed so implausible. I would need to look out for him on the dock side, but when the Aurelia arrived in Hawaii and the ship was buzzing with excitement, our disembarkation was delayed. The news came in the form of a tannoy announcement which advised all passengers that a small matter of business had to be taken care of prior to the gates opening.

I had my suspicions as to what the small matter might be, but I didn't have to work hard to get them confirmed because the news spread around the ship before most people got off: The FBI had arrested Bhavana.

The two FBI agents, who had been on board since Los Angeles, had to wait until the ship returned to American waters to make their arrest and did so very publicly, taking Bhavana into custody as she left her suite. She screamed bloody murder as they read her rights, then came to her senses, demanded a lawyer and clamped her mouth firmly shut. Though Ian Kenyon was dead and couldn't testify, it soon came out that while we were all at sea, one of her other victims had finally broken down and confessed to his wife. It was the one tactic that was guaranteed to release her hold. His wife forgave him but then insisted he step forward and expose the truth about Bhavana's methods. He was a very rich, very influential Hollywood Director and once he spoke out, so did several others, opening a virtual floodgate like Harvey Weinstein in reverse.

It was in the paper by the time I got hold of one later that day and though I wondered if her lawyers would get her off the hook, it seemed likely her movie career was done. Her future wasn't something I cared about; I was too busy dreaming about mine.

The End

Don't miss the extract from the next book – <u>The Couple in Cabin 2124</u> which you can find just a couple of pages down.

Note from the author:

I finished editing and correcting this book a few days after attending an independent author's convention in Edinburgh. I had been writing in utter isolation for five years and had never met another author, so to find more than two hundred of them all gathered in one place was quite something. I learned a lot about the industry and about marketing and about how to attract new readers, but the thing that stuck with me is how much I love what I do.

There will come a point in the next couple of years, when I will transition from my life as a part-time author with a full-time job, to a new life as a full-time author and I cannot wait. Writing stories is the thing I would choose to do above anything else. Yes, even including that thing you are now thinking. At the moment, I rise at five o'clock each morning to write, forcing time into my day where none would otherwise exist. I write for two hours, then cross my garden to a log cabin where I have a gym. I'm an advocate of CrossFit, a combination of cardiovascular exercise and weightlifting performed at speed which ensures I stay fit and healthy; something I need since I am nearing fifty and have a three-year-old son. I then cycle to work, a distance of roughly eight miles, put in ten or more hours, then cycle home, play with my son, give him a bath and put him to bed. By half past eight it is time to feed myself, but an hour later I kiss my wife as she retires to read in bed, and I begin writing again. Usually, I give in a little after midnight and the cycle repeats the next day. If you are feeling sympathy for me, then please do not: I feel blessed, I am intensely privileged to be able to do what I do and have people tell me they enjoyed it.

The characters I create come from somewhere deep inside me. Patricia, in particular, has become a part of my life and I will admit that I have shed an occasional tear as I plot out how her story will end. Not because it is sad, which I would never do to my readers, but because it is so amazing. She is already rising from the shrivelled form she had become, stuck inside a marriage that reduced her to a shadow of the vibrant young woman she once was. Now, the real Patricia is emerging as her inner strength returns and by the time the ship finally returns to England... well, I guess you will have to keep reading. I promise you this though, the remining books in the series will give you more of exactly what you already love.

As I type these last few words, it is almost ten o'clock on a Thursday night on the day after The Kidnapped Bride was published. This book is done and about to be uploaded to the sales platform, so in a minute or so, I can get back to Patricia's next adventure. Honestly, I can't wait.

If you wish to support my efforts, the best way you can do that is by leaving a review on Amazon. Reviews are important because prospective readers discovering me for the first time want to hear from other readers, not the author. No more than a few words is required. If you wish to do this, just click the link: The Director's Cut

This is not my first series though; there are many other books already waiting for you. So, if you enjoy Patricia's adventures, you may wish to check out **Tempest Michaels**, **Amanda Harper** and **Jane Butterworth**. Like Patricia, they solve mysteries and their stories are written to make you laugh and keep you turning pages when you really ought to be going to sleep.

Finally, there is a **Patricia Fisher** story that you may not yet have found. It is part of this series but sits apart from it. It is called *Killer Cocktail* and you can have it for free. Just click the link below and tell me where to send it.

Yes! Send me my FREE Patricia Fisher story!

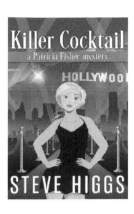

An Evening Stroll Ruined

The sun was slowly setting over the port quarter of the ship's nose as I took a quiet walk around the ship. I did this most nights before retiring with a book, it helped me to order my thoughts and commit as many of the wonderful things I had seen and experienced to memory. It was the height of summer now and I was almost halfway through my around the world cruise, a fact which both pleased and saddened at the same time.

That I had been able to take this trip in the first place ought to be a sore subject, but it wasn't. My husband had cheated on me and my flight from that situation had led me to take up residence in the Royal Suite of the world's finest luxury cruise ship. Since then, my life had become a whirlwind of adventure, exotic places and incredible experiences. The only element I could possibly be unhappy about was having no one to share it with. I had been married for thirty years, walking down the aisle at just nineteen when I had met *the one* and was happily swept off my feet. Three decades later, the shine had left the marriage along with any physical affection and the vibrant young girl I had been was buried beneath the shroud of a middle-aged woman with no purpose and no perceptible joy.

The ship was currently bound for Japan where it would dock in Tokyo for two days. The passage from Hawaii was the second longest of the trip unavoidably because there was nothing between Hawaii and Japan apart from a vast expanse of Pacific Ocean. Now, almost exactly four days into that leg, I was ready to get off an explore again when we docked tomorrow lunchtime. I had a niggling concern that my estranged husband might show up, but every time the thought raised its head, I knocked it back down with a derisory laugh. Charlie never went anywhere. It was a fact that had angered me for most of our marriage but was now something I could rely on. A week ago, he had called me in my cabin and promised to meet me in Hawaii. He hadn't showed of course, but the niggling doubt remained because, despite years of avoiding planes and travel, he had been waiting for me in St Kitts when the ship docked there. I had avoided him then, even though I knew he was coming and had agreed to meet with him to discuss our future, but now I wasn't sure what he might do.

One thing was for sure, I had moved on. The forced time apart had allowed me to shrug off the shroud and rediscover myself hiding beneath it. The vibrancy returned almost overnight, so that I now felt excited each morning by the prospect of the day ahead.

Then there was the captain to consider.

I didn't get to focus my thoughts on Captain Alistair Huntley's handsome features though because I reached the stern of the enormous ship and came across a sight that cleared my mind of everything else: there was a man climbing over the railings.

'Hey,' I called out. Then again louder, 'Hey!' as I continued to walk toward him. I looked around but there was no one else about. It was late, so the passengers would be in bars or restaurants or in the many theatres, cinemas or clubs the great ship boasted. It was probably why the man had chosen this time to come up here and the dread feeling telling me he was on his way to commit suicide became a definite when I saw the weight he was carrying in one hand.

I dashed to the railing at the very back of the ship, but unwilling to climb over as he had, I tried calling yet again. This time he heard me and turned his head. The mask of pain his face betrayed broke my heart instantly and I wondered what I could possibly say that might convince

175

him to reconsider. I didn't have to present an argument for life though because he instantly started back toward me.

Beyond the railing at the very back of the ship were steel mesh panels reaching upward to a height of around three yards and the same panels extended outwards supported on steel girders so the man was currently walking on them directly above the maelstrom of water being churned up by the ship's propellers.

I didn't know, but it was my assumption that the mesh panels were there to provide some kind of maintenance access to something. I was fairly certain though that they were not meant to be accessed while at sea. Despite the man's mask of misery, he made his way back from the edge to the other side of the mesh separating us. My heart was thumping in my chest but beginning to calm down. That was until he stopped. I expected him to start climbing; to be depressed enough about his life to contemplate suicide but to have changed his mind the moment he saw someone take an interest.

Instead, he dug around in a pocket to pull out a crumpled note, then he grabbed the mesh, his fingers curling through it right next to where I was also holding it so that his skin touched mine in several places. 'You're Patricia Fisher, aren't you?' he said. It was a question, but I felt that he already knew the answer before I nodded. He looked up to the sky at that point as if having an argument with God.

When he looked back down, I said, 'Please come back onto the ship. It's not safe out there. You don't want to do this.' The weight I spotted earlier was tied around his waist with a belt. It was a round disc that he must have taken from one of the gyms and looked to weight fifty pounds or more. With it tied to him, he would sink like a rock.

The man looked squarely at me as he replied, 'It's too late for me.'

'No, it isn't,' I pleaded, trying to get through to him. 'We can work through this.'

He just shook his head. Then he thrust the note through the mesh and into my hand as he yelled, 'You have to save Anna. Nothing else matters. I've caused too much harm already. I jump now or they kill me tomorrow.' I stared blankly at him, trying to think of something I could say, but nothing came. 'Save Anna!' he yelled once more then he let go of the railing, turned and started running.

A panicked gasp escaped my lips as fear for what I was about to see filled my belly. I screamed, 'No!' at his back and had to watch as he reached the end of the platform and jumped, the weight held in his hands and against his body as he fell. I don't think my heart bothered to beat in the time it took for him to fall and hit the churning surf below. Then he was gone. Gone forever, swallowed by the restless waves as, unknowingly, the ship continued onwards to its destination.

I heaved in ragged gulps of air as I continued to stare at the spot where he had entered the water. I knew of course, that had he somehow bobbed back to the surface, he would have been hundreds of yards behind the ship already as it thrust itself forward at close to forty knots.

When my heartrate started to slow, I looked about again but there was still no one in sight. What I did spot though was a man-over-board alarm. It was a large red button with an even larger red sign above it. I knew there was nothing anyone could do for the man, but I pressed it anyway and then slumped to the cold deck to wait for the ship's security team to arrive.

Get the full book by clicking this link: The Couple in Cabin 2124

Printed in Great Britain
by Amazon

67519600R00109